War in Siberia

Friends Parted

DAVID WORDLEY WILLIAMS

To Celia Heritage
for giving life to
The Williams Family

David W. Williams

Ⓒ
THE CHOIR PRESS

First published in the United Kingdom in 2023 by
The Choir Press

ISBN 978-1-78963-396-2

Drafts of the maps, graphics and book cover were originated by the author but developed and made ready for print by graphic designer Terry Ayling.

DISCLAIMER

This book is dedicated to
Judith Mary Williams
26th July 1937 to 29th July 2021
My wife of 61 years and so missed

And to
The officers commissioned into the Royal Engineers on
4th February 1955, following cadetship at the Royal Military
Academy, Sandhurst, as the 14th intake following the
then recent war.
Thank you for your company.

Finally, my thanks to Sylvia Robus, who patiently and diligently
edited and transcribed an almost unintelligible manuscript
to type.
Thank you.

War in Siberia

This book is a work of fiction, but …

It is based on two historic facts, with the narrative weaving together:

1. The consequences of the Treaties of Aigun (1858) and Peking (1860) which led to the annexation by Russia of over a million square kilometres of Chinese land in eastern Siberia: called an unfair treaty by China, and
2. The annexation of Crimea by Russia in 2014 and failures in Ukraine following its invasion in 2022. China then decides to protect its strategic interests by moving into eastern Siberia.

This book provides a narrative whereby China regains its lost territory from Russia which loses its empire. The time frame, facts and events will change but the end result is considered to be ultimately inevitable.

The Author

勿 忘 国 耻

咸丰签准《北京条约》处

1860年10月28日（九月十五乙巳），咸丰皇帝在此殿西暖阁被迫签准同英、法、俄的《北京条约》，将香港对岸的南九龙割让给英国。承认《爱晖条约》中，将黑龙江以北，乌苏里江以东一百多万平方公里领土割让俄国的丧权辱国条款有效。

NO FORGETTING THE NATIONAL HUMILIATION
Emperor Xianfeng signed Beijing Treaty here

On October 28,1860(September 15 by lunar calendar),it was in the warm chamber Xianfeng was forced to sign Beijing Treaty with Britain, France and Russia which ceded south Kowloon to Britain and to admit Aihui Treaty through which more than 1000000 square kilometer territory that lies to the north of the Heilongjiang river and to the east of Wusulijiang river was ceded to Russia .

Picture of the Memorial Stone where Beijing Treaty was signed.

This Book

This book presents a narrative piecing together events linked to Russia's invasion of Ukraine with consequences that stir China into action to protect its strategic interests. These include the protection of its northern border with Russia's Siberia and the recovery of the million or so square kilometres of Siberian land annexed by Russia following the Treaty of Aigun.

The narrative links news items posted by our correspondents and editors with verbatim reports of newsworthy items released by other organisations and commentaries released by Chinese (China Forward) and UK (New Europe)-based think tanks. Personal experiences of participants in the military actions covered are also included.

Contents

Moscow to Vladivostock is 9300kms by road or rail. Siberia from east to west spans 13 time zones.

MANCHURIA - RUSSIA BOUNDARY

RUSSIA

Russian-Chinese border after 1860

Sea of Okhotsk

Albezino (Albazin)

Tugur

Nerchinsk

Ceded to Russia by the treaty of Aigun 1858

Belogorsk

Komsomol'sk

SAKHALIN

Blagoveshchensk

Chiu-ai-hun (Aigun)

Russian-Chinese border according to the Treaty of Nerchinsk 1689

MANCHURIA (CHINA)

Khabarovsk

Ceded to Russia by the Peking Conference 1860

Harbin

Ch'ang ch'un

JAPAN

0   100   200 miles

Vladivostok

Sea of Japan

Land annexed by Russia from China
1858, Treaty of Aigun   1860, Peaking Conference

UKRAINE BEFORE RUSSIAN INVASION OF FEBRUARY 2014

Preface to War in Siberia – China claims its Lost Province

The war between Russia and Ukraine, started by the former, remains unresolved. There exists an insurmountable gap between Ukraine's desire to regain lost territory and the Russian President's overwhelming desire to regain lost imperial lands. Russia has already lost significant face in failing to make any worthwhile gain, given its fluctuating objectives, fighting an army much smaller than its own and losing a significant proportion of the combat forces it deployed. It has also lost current and long-term financial and economic well-being and created, inevitable at some point, an impoverished and discontented population. Russia has shown itself to be much weaker than international opinion had assumed. In particular, its much-vaulted partnership with China has been seen to be very unbalanced, given that its economic muscle is only about one-tenth of China's and demonstrated by China's lukewarm response to Russia's call for support and in particular its initial withholding of offensive material. This situation has created a potentially dangerous position for Russia, controlling the whole of Siberia, with eleven time zones between Moscow and Vladivostok, and with very meagre economic resources to develop and protect such a huge area. It borders with Kazakhstan and Mongolia to the south and the very powerful economic and military power of China south of eastern Siberia. A long-existing and potentially very serious border dispute arises as a consequence of the terms of the Treaty of Aigun 1858 and the Convention of Peking, signed in 1860 which, signed under the threat of overwhelming Russian military presence, assigned to Russia over one million square kilometres of Chinese territory north of the River Amur and east of the River Ussuri. China regards this as an unequal treaty, agreed under duress.

As part of the Convention of Peking, China ceded territory to Great Britain (Hong Kong), Portugal (Macau) and free trade rights to France, Germany, the USA and Japan, along the South China Sea, centred on Shanghai. These aspects of the period of unequal treaties were resolved as a consequence of World War II and by later agreement with the countries involved. The unequal treaty forced on China by Russia remains. Given the circumstances outlined above, the narrative postulates that China believes that the time has come to reverse the terms of the treaty.

Russian East Siberia has become a boil on the carcass of a rotten state, waiting to be lanced by China. This narrative describes the potential achievement of that goal.

The Aigun Treaty – Historical Background

Russia is the largest country in the world; Siberia makes up most of its land area, with eleven time zones between Moscow and Vladivostok. Russia sits at one end of this vast area whilst China sits at the other. Each country knew very little of the other until approximately the seventeenth century: the first Russian known to have visited Peking did so in 1614.

The first state interaction was prompted by Russian Cossacks, adventurers and traders moving east through Siberian forests following the River Amur, generally avoiding the warlike Oirat tribes living in more northern parts of Siberia. These Cossacks and other Russians eventually reached the Amur Basin and the shores of the north Pacific in 1643. At that time, the Manchus of the Chinese Empire held loose sovereignty over the whole of the eastern part of Siberia. The Chinese regarded the Russian arrivals as vagabonds and buccaneers, creating a nuisance in their territory, which was very casually and ineffectively governed. Finally, the Chinese authorities lost patience with the Russian invaders and, after the Battle of Albazin 1685, drove them back to west of the Stanovoy Mountains. The Russians gave up the Amur Basin but kept land between the Argun River and Lake Baikal. The boundary to the west of the Stanovoy Mountains and south of the Argun River, to Lake Baikal and the Amur River, was to remain the boundary between Russia and China until the Treaty of Aigun in 1858. However, China continued to question the validity of Russia's presence and refused trade between the two countries until the border issue was resolved.

China defeated the Oirat Khanate at the battle of Ulan Bator in 1690 and took control of Inner Mongolia, followed by Outer Mongolia in 1696. This led to disputes with Russia regarding its northern border. This dispute with Peter the Great led to the Treaty of Kyakhta in 1729. Post-1729, China annexed Xinjiang; Russia acquired Kazakhstan. The Russia/China border now met at East Kazakhstan and Western Xinjiang. Russia also annexed the Kamchatka Peninsular. Following these territorial movements, trade problems between both powers were resolved in the Treaty of Kulgam in 1851.

The Treaty of Aigun 1858–59

By 1848, China was in an extremely weak condition, economically and militarily. It was trying to control the Taiping Rebellion, was involved in the Opium Wars and was being oppressed, particularly by British and French military pressures on its southern coastline. The British and French attacked and partly destroyed parts of Peking. Russia had built up a military force of tens of thousands of troops in its Siberian territory, north of China, which was in so much turmoil that it hardly noticed. Russia knew that China was losing the Opium Wars and its local commander resolved to restore Russia to its lands east of the Stanovoy Mountains, lost in the late 1690s. The Chinese Governor of East Siberia had no military force available and was forced to accede to Russian demands. The Treaty of Aigun was signed on behalf of the Qing dynasty in Argun. The treaty ceded territory bounded by the River Ussuri to the west, the Amur to the south and the Sea of Japan to the east. In all, this amounted to six hundred thousand square kilometres of northern Manchuria. At the same time, Britain and France extorted major concessions from China, including tariff-free treaty ports and trade and legal protection of the rights of foreigners. These rights were included in the Treaty of Tientsin. Rights gained by Russia and European powers were confirmed in the Convention of Peking in 1860, which also gave further rights to Russia, including total control of the Pacific coastline to Korea at Vladivostok. The Island of Sakhalin was ceded to Russia and Japan. As a consequence of the Treaty of Aigun and the Peking Convention, Russia gained a total of over one million square kilometres of Chinese land.

These arrangements amounted to a very large transfer of land and economic and legal rights from China to foreign powers and were henceforth labelled as unfair treaties by China. In 1927, China expressed its desire to obtain at least a partial reversal of the terms of Aigun, but the proposal was put into abeyance by the invasion of China by Japan.

Footnote

In 1969, China and Russia engaged in a significant military confrontation along the Ussuri River. At that time, China was much the weaker power and, as a so-called gesture of good will, it reaffirmed its acceptance of the Treaty of Aigun and a truce was declared. This gesture would not be taken seriously if a dispute arose again.

From the early seventeenth century to the period leading up to the Aigun Treaty, the relationship between Russia and China was one of constant confrontation. This was sometimes local or diplomatic but frequently military. The states were ill balanced: Russia part of a rapidly industrialising West and China, riven by internal conflict, was economically and militarily weak and in no position to defend itself against predatory external states.

Hence Aigun.

CHAPTER ONE

Russia has Problems in Ukraine

The Russian Army is exhausted. Civil unrest in the Donbas. A Russian commander complains and the Russian President stops missile strikes on Ukrainian infrastructure.

Russia has Problems

By our Defence Editor

The Truce

Russia and Ukraine have battled themselves to a standstill and a truce is finally arranged. The President's army had managed to occupy a significant part of the Donbas. He still called his war a 'Special Military Operation' and in so doing, saved himself the embarrassment of calling his action a war, potentially involving the whole Russian population. However, he deprived himself of the advantages of national mobilisation. Such an action would have allowed the call-up of reserves, diversion of manufacturing capability to military hardware and moving finance away from social projects. None of this would have been popular or even acceptable to the Russian population. He began to feel the limits of his popularity and power. Having partially succeeded in the Donbas, he could at least claim victory. This victory was a far cry from his original ambitions but could be dressed up by propaganda to seem like a success. His battered army needed a respite to allow retraining, re-equipping and morale boosting to meet his continuing aim of occupying more Ukrainian land. Russia's ability to re-equip itself had been lessened by a historic decline of manufacturing capability and the effects of sanctions. He placed some faith in the prospect of material help from China and Belarus. To get to this point, he had been forced to accept ceasefire terms which prevented further rocket or missile attacks on Ukraine from any source. He was also aware of

Patriot anti-missile systems on Ukrainian territory. He accepted that
non-observation of this aspect of the terms would bring about NATO
offensive air strikes. It was also agreed, after intense international pressure,
that Ukraine would commence export of grain from Odesa, coordinated by
Turkey. Ukraine, which by now had recaptured Kherson, had not given up
its ambition to recover land seized by Russia, including Crimea. Ukraine
was content to go along with this truce as it allowed it to rebuild its military,
especially including training in the use of an increasing flow of allied
weaponry. The truce also allowed the continued export of grain, so
important to its farmers and national economy and to many countries,
especially in Asia and North Africa, needing to feed their populations.

Civil Unrest

At this time, war had cost the lives of at least twenty-five thousand
Ukrainian civilians. A far cry from the pretended intention of the Russian
President to rescue the Ukrainian people from the control of Nazis. He
continued his pretence of welcoming the Ukrainian population back into
'mother' Russia by holding a referendum on the absorption of Donbas and
Southern Ukraine, which was approved by an unbelievable 99% of the
population. Russian passports were issued and Russian roubles introduced
as the local currency. The payment of salaries by the Ukrainian
Government to surviving national employees was stopped. In the Donbas,
food and petrol supplies to civilians became precarious and military/police
control became oppressive. Economic and social movement across the new
borders was banned. The consequence of this environment was growing
discontent. Contact between the Russian occupiers and the local
population became hostile and non-cooperative in both directions. Street
demonstrations became increasingly frequent, well attended and disruptive
of normal civilian and military routine. The terms of the truce, in theory,
banned heavy-handed displays of force to subdue street protests, but the
protests became increasingly violent and impossible to contain with normal
crowd control. Images of the protests and inevitable heavy-handed restraint
found their way onto western television and social IT channels and also
onto the Donbas and Russian networks. This was not good advertising as a
backup for the Russian President's reassuring message to his public. In
reality, the truce was the start of a chain of events which would eventually
unwind all of the President's plans for the establishment of a Russian
Empire.

Unrest in the Donbas

By our Kyiv Correspondent

Communications within units of the Russian invading force had been seen to be very poorly managed, based on inadequate and outdated equipment. Interception of messages on mobile phone networks initiated by lower ranks became routine. Such messages frequently highlighted the poor levels of information available to them and advertised their poor state of morale. Messages exchanged by more senior ranks were intercepted less frequently but were still a constant source of intelligence on troop movements, tactical plans and logistic problems. The particular message paraphrased below falls into this category and was released by Ukraine's military headquarters in Kyiv.

A Situation Report

By a combat commander, identified as a Colonel Sergei Orlov, to his brigade commander in Severodonetsk.

> You have given me responsibility for the protection of our units in Severodonetsk and Lysychansk, and for controlling any civil unrest arising in these cities. So far as our soldiers are concerned, I repeat problems mentioned before about the poor quantity of the rations we receive and also about the lack of medical facilities. Many of my soldiers have received no leave since the start of the campaign. I hope this position can be corrected soon. My main concern is that partisan attacks on my units are occurring more frequently. These attacks seem to be carried out by individuals. I have lost three personnel carriers in four days. The standard method of attack is to place anti-tank mines on the engine covers of my vehicles, which are detonated by remote control. This leads to total destruction of the vehicle. Guarding all our vehicles at night is not possible given the small number of infantry at my disposal. My five hundred infantry soldiers have to mount street patrols plus guarding the sensitive locations we control. This is an impossible task given the wide area concerned. I have also lost five soldiers in the same period. They were off duty and drinking in local cafés, but their deaths

reflect the very hostile reception we have met in moving around the city. There are almost daily demonstrations of up to five hundred people, which are quite difficult to control given the few soldiers I have available. On three occasions, we have been forced to use tear gas and fire live shots into the air. It seems to me that we will need to use targeted live fire unless many more troops or police are brought in to control the population. I do not feel able to adequately control the situation with my limited present resources and ask for assistance as quickly as possible.

CHAPTER TWO

Combatant Experiences

Five stories told by servicemen caught up in the Ukrainian War.

A conversation with Dimitri Luckashoshoko

A view expressed by Major Oscar Bulganin

An event described by Major Stepan Stavinsky

A partisan at war by Ivanov Bassky

A Russian soldier has problems Private Kozlov Rosscoff

A record of a conversation with Dimitri Luckashoshoko

Recorded by our Kyiv Correspondent

I am a lieutenant in the 2nd Battalion of the 4th Infantry Brigade in the Ukrainian Army. In normal life, I am a car mechanic but on 24th February 2022, immediately after the invasion of Ukraine by Russia, I volunteered at the Kyiv Military Headquarters for active service. I had served as a part-time soldier over the past three years and needed very little updating training. I was immediately sent to join my battalion, which was on the existing front line near Donetsk. This front line had existed since Russia annexed Crimea and part of the Donbas oblast in 2014. Our front line consisted of four trenches dug to about two metres deep and separated by about twenty metres of cleared ground. Each trench included a reverse corner every fifteen metres so that damage caused by a shell exploding in the trench was limited by the solid earth wall at each bend in the trench line. Each fifteen-metre trench section included a dugout on the enemy side, raised from the trench floor to limit flooding and revetted with timber on the sides and ceiling to prevent earth slip. The dugouts would accept two men and were fitted with straw-filled canvas mattresses used by men off duty. Sandbags lined the trench top on the enemy side to provide rests for rifles and machine guns. The enemy included a few Russian conscripts but were mostly militia recruited from the Russian- speaking civil Donbas population. We were, in fact, fighting fellow Ukrainians of the wrong sort.

Activity after 2014 had been low level, but our own war finally woke up on 27th February 2022, following the Russian invasion. The enemy (called the Russians from now on) had their own trench line about eight hundred metres from our own. The battalion armourer had acquired DIY drones from Kyiv and had fitted these with cameras. They had a range of about one kilometre and, so far, the Russians had not thought it necessary to shoot them down. Therefore, we could see that a significant Russian armoured presence was building up behind their lines.

We could deploy only two T72 tanks which were dug in and camouflaged about half a kilometre behind our position. Our main defensive activity and hope rested on our NLAW hand-held anti-tank rocket launchers of which we held one every fifteen metres of trench. We were grateful for this gift from the British. Every time we fired one, we called out, "God Save the Queen."

The attack on our position was preceded by fifty rounds of artillery shellfire. In later attacks, the Russians fired hundreds of rounds, but at this time they did not anticipate any worthwhile resistance from us and relied on the traditional Russian tactic of overwhelming their enemy by attacking in strength.

Dozens of T72 tanks attacked across the battalion front, supported by a small group of infantry behind each tank and more infantry mounted in armoured infantry personnel carriers. Our NLAW anti-tank weapons had a range of about eight hundred metres. Once the image finder was locked on a target, the weapon activated its own guidance system. The heavy shaped charge warhead exploded on side or top impact and was lethal enough to penetrate any armour and explode inside the vehicle. By this time, our operatives were well trained and the weapons assured high success rates against armoured vehicles. The resultant destruction of leading tanks was a very welcome sight to those of us fearing attack tanks passing over our heads. Within thirty minutes, all the attack tanks had been destroyed or retired. T72 tanks carry their ammunition in a magazine stored inside the turret. Almost always, the striking missile ignited the stored ammunition, resulting in the turret being blown two to three metres into the air, followed by what remained of the crew. Follow-up medical facilities were not generally required. Having disposed of the T72 tanks, our NLAW firers turned on the personnel carriers. These had advanced to within fifty metres of our positions and disgorged their infantry, who rushed our positions. Each personnel carrier dismounted a mortar, which went into action quite quickly and caused a number of casualties. The remaining intact vehicles also laid down a barrage of 30mm shellfire onto our trenches.

We had been in our defensive positions for many months and had constructed barbed wire entanglements in front of our trenches. One or two attacking personnel carriers attempted to cross our wire but quickly became entangled, with wire jammed in their tracks. Dismounted infantry attempted to cross our wire, but this was impossible and many were killed. In later attacks, we suffered from artillery barrages which destroyed much of our entanglements but still made them very difficult to cross. The situation seemed very similar to conditions in the First World War which I had seen on film. The Russians did not seem too concerned about their dead soldiers and we found ourselves clearing bodies from in front of our trenches and burning them in unused trenches in our own areas.

The battlefield was now a chaotic scene of burning armoured vehicles, attack troops bravely trying to reach our lines and mayhem as we fought off the attacking soldiers and attended to those of us who had been injured in the prolonged assault. In the end, our defences were not penetrated.

The Russian attackers suffered very significant losses of armour and soldiers with minimum loss to ourselves. We are aware that the Russian attack had been based on an expectation of minimum resistance by ourselves and an arrogant assumption of their own superiority. We sustained many attacks over the next few weeks. Such attacks generally followed the same principle of mass assault, the Russians seemingly having learnt very little from the disaster of their initial attack. However, a significant difference was that each future attack was preceded by a sustained artillery barrage which caused us many casualties. We also had to change our tactics – but that is another story.

A Viewpoint Expressed by Major Oscar Bulganin

Second-In-Command of First Infantry Battalion 5th Ukrainian Army Infantry Brigade

Recorded by our Correspondent somewhere west of Severodonetsk

We are glad of a break from the front line which we have been in or close to since the Russian invasion of 24th February 2022. This battalion is a regular unit which was one of the first to meet the Russian advance. We started out with seven hundred and fifty men. Half of that number have since been killed or wounded. We have received replacement numbers, mostly only partially trained but they learn on the job and by experiencing the very heavy weight of firepower the Russians throw at us. The only tactic known to the Russians appears to be massive direct assault. When we are in open country, they come at us with combined tank and personnel carrier assault, with the infantry dismounting at the last moment. For us, this was a bit of a turkey shoot because we were well stocked with anti-tank missiles provided by the USA, Britain and Germany, which were very accurate and in which we had been well trained. Russian losses were very high; tanks seemed to be very vulnerable to our missiles and suffered very major damage after strikes, frequently as a consequence of the secondary damage to the vehicles caused by the detonation of their ammunition magazines. Seeing the mayhem caused amongst their tanks, the infantry armoured vehicles tend to retire rather than suffer the same fate. Dismounted infantry seldom get near our wire-protected trenches and are then disposed of without difficulty. In urban areas, tanks were seldom used after initial assaults as they suffered too many casualties from NLAWs, ambushed at close quarters. There is generally a shortage of infantry in the Russian combat groups, leading to inadequate support for lead echelons which consequently make little progress.

Having failed in their preliminary tactics, they then switched to a reliance on artillery, and that tactic certainly caused us much more trouble. I have read my history books and I recall a disastrous episode in the history of the British Empire and, in particular, an event at Spion Kop. A British battalion had created a scrape trench line, intended for temporary occupation along a ridge line; Spion Kop. Boers brought up artillery and shelled the ridge line. The battalion stayed for too long in their exposed position with totally inadequate trenches and were very virtually wiped out. The Russians knew where we were and we could not effectively move without surrendering our position. This situation occurred frequently. The Russian Army has always been artillery heavy and a routine tactic is to engage an enemy position with a heavy and prolonged artillery barrage, immediately preceding an armoured or infantry attack. We are at least better prepared than Spion Kop, with deep revetted trenches with overhead cover. Nevertheless, sitting through a bombardment was a frightening experience. A direct hit would be instant death, which was not all that encouraging. At this period, I believe that the Ukrainian Army was losing at least a hundred men a day in these circumstances.

Much respite was provided once USA- and British-supplied multi-barrel rocket launchers, GPS guided, became available to attack the Russian artillery. The accuracy and destructive power of these units provided huge relief. The superior capability of western and NATO equipment compared with the somewhat obsolete Russian material is apparent. The problem is that not enough is available. Nevertheless, our ability to strike back with such power was very good for morale.

I repeat the message broadcast by our president that Ukraine is quite capable of defeating the Russian Army deployed in Ukraine, given adequate material support from our NATO allies.

An event in The Life of Major Stepan Stavinsky

Recorded by our Kyiv Correspondent

I work in the IT department of the Ukrainian Army Headquarters in Kyiv. I assess our own intelligence inputs and the GPS intelligence provided by the USA. I provide reports to the General Staff on activities in areas of particular interest on the battlefield. I also coordinate the activities of intelligence-seeking drones provided by the USA and offensively armed drones bought from Turkey. Prior to the 24th of February 2022, Russia and Belarus joint military exercises had taken place in southern Belarus. On 24th February, Belarus became party to the invasion of Ukraine by allowing Russian columns to move across its southern border into Ukraine. Russian forces made significant gains in northern Ukraine in the first two weeks of the war, including the capture of Chernobyl nuclear power station. Forces moving on the main roads from Belarus to Kyiv thereafter made slow progress against determined Ukrainian resistance. The central thrust of the

Russian columns was headed to Kyiv. A principal task given to the invading force was the capture of Kyiv in the expectation of installing a puppet government able to declare the end of hostilities and of the war. A column of about four hundred tanks, other armoured vehicles and logistic and repair vehicles, set out on their southern journey to Kyiv. The column consisted of a mixture of combat and logistic vehicles and was many kilometres long. Russia had expected the columns to move smoothly, greeted by welcoming support from the alleged oppressed civil population. In fact, progress was hard fought against fierce Ukrainian Army resistance, and Russian optimism faded, confronted with the self-induced problems they encountered. The weather was bad. Any off-road movement was difficult but necessary to allow for bivouac areas, passing places, storage dumps, rest areas and to allow for breakdowns and recovery. The columns bunched, blocking the roads. The combat units more or less ground to a halt. This led to very difficult conditions for logistic resupply vehicles attempting to travel the length of the stalled column. Fuel supplies did not get through and vehicles halted where they were, unable to advance. Ammunition resupply was very difficult and food supplies to the thousands of soldiers marooned along the column did not get through either, resulting in hungry soldiers with low morale having been very poorly briefed on their purpose. They had been led to believe that they were part of a continuing training exercise amongst a friendly population. Of more interest to our military was how poorly the column was defended. My section launched three drones from the military airfield north of Kyiv. I guided them directly onto a suitable target. There was no Russian air cover, and no small arms or canon fire from the ground. The first drone sent target information to me, visible on my screen. From a height of about five hundred metres, I released the first drone's 5kg warhead onto the southernmost tank. The missile hit it in its centre. The detonation of the missile itself was followed within twenty seconds by a much larger explosion as the ammunition magazine in the tank blew up. My second drone was then aimed at the rear tank of the same group, with the same effect. My third drone was in reserve, should either of the first two fail. To add to the conflagration, I aimed it at a fuel tanker in the centre of the column. The vehicle blew up with an enormous explosion.

Prepositioned Ukrainian infantry, in ambush on both sides of the road, now fired their anti-tank rockets into the sides of the immobile vehicles. Towering columns of flame and smoke enveloped the whole convoy. Every armoured vehicle and petrol tanker in the group of vehicles I had selected was destroyed. Apart from the loss of these vehicles, their wreckage now created an even greater obstacle. The Russian column was heavy in terms of armoured vehicles – tanks and personnel carriers – but poorly provided with infantry capable of protecting its flanks against ambush attack. The Ukrainian infantry made full use of this tactical error and preyed on the column once it had stopped moving. On this same day in early March, I also identified a section of another column, made up of twelve tanks and five personnel carriers, interspersed with five fuel tankers, parked on a road in a woodland area stretching along about two kilometres of road backed by minor roads and open country. I was aware of GPS information which showed that there was no covering infantry protection either side of the road. The approach from the south for our own troops appeared to be clear of enemy. A simple plan involved infantry moving up to the west of the wood in personnel carriers, then moving through the wood to the column on the road, with arrival timed to coincide with an armed drone strike which I was able to coordinate from my office in Kyiv. Our drones had a range of seventy-five kilometres and could loiter in the air for up to two hours. My section engaged the column with drones as it had earlier in the day. Again, the entire column was destroyed. The ambushing infantry retreated back into the woods and returned to their vehicles. The Russian column had not fired a single shot in return. Most of the Russian soldiers were bivouacked clear of the road but there must have been significant casualties, and their losses on that day helped compromise their assault on Kyiv. The attacking force had been simply overconfident and paid for it on this day and after other attacks arranged on subsequent days.

Russian losses in armour on this and following days by armed drones introduced a new battlefield weapon, which called into question the nature of tank warfare, but in the near term, I was happy for them to stick with their current tactics.

A Partisan at War – Ivanov Bassky of Kherson

Recounted to and recorded by our Correspondent

I am a butcher by trade and have lived in Kherson all my life. During the last week in February 2022, Russian soldiers began to arrive in Kherson. They seemed to have met very little resistance and my friends here suggested that some of our leaders, of Russian extraction and sympathy, may have aided their arrival. All my friends and a large majority of the city population found this outrageous and planned some sort of uprising. Many Ukrainian flags appeared across the city, and small demonstrations were held when Russian vehicles appeared. Our mayor was arrested, although later released, and a local Russian sympathiser appointed in his place. Ukrainian army units remained within twenty kilometres of the city. The front line between these units and the Russians in the city was very lightly patrolled, especially by the Russians. A group of men who formed themselves into a self-defence militia unit were quickly in touch with the Ukrainian units nearby. We were all optimistic and assumed that Kherson could be freed before too long. We decided to help along that process by biting at the heels of the Russians within the city area. The Russian garrison was quite small; probably no more than five hundred men. We did not feel too restrained in moving about the city.

We were supplied with rifles and anti-tank and anti-personnel mines from our nearby army units. Our first effective direct attacks were aimed at soft targets, such as logistic vehicles parked in the streets. At night, it was relatively easy to throw a petrol bomb into the back of a truck. This produced a very nice fire very quickly. We moved on to placing anti-tank mines under vehicle wheels or tracks of armoured vehicles. They lost a few before realising how vulnerable they were, being forced to check their vehicles before they moved. We knew where they assembled for parades and checkpoint handovers. We therefore embarked on other more hazardous tasks of ambushing some of these assemblies, causing short-lived small arms firefights before disappearing into the alleyways and built-up areas which we knew so well. We were not able to stay at these sites for very long, but we caused casualties and they became very wary before venturing out far from their bases. Our actions also served to display the anger of the people of Kherson at the Russian presence and kept within the city an infantry unit which might have caused trouble to the Ukrainian Army elsewhere. There are about eleven men in our group: one accountant, two car mechanics, two medical orderlies, two from the local supermarket, two from a holiday agency, one from an optician's and myself. There are at least ten other groups like ourselves, all armed and willing to fight. The groups will combine to attack the Russian garrison when the Ukrainian Army comes back. At night, we go out in groups of three, hunting single soldiers, probably drunk, which many of them are, and 'disposing' of them. We never use weapons, which would give away our presence, and instead endeavour to leave what looks like the scene of an accident. This lowers the risk of any reprisals from the Russians. Every 'disposal' is one less to fight our army.

A Russian Soldier with Problems:
Private Kozlov Rosscoff

Recorded by our Correspondent: Kyiv

Russian soldiers typically use their iPhone equivalent to talk to their relatives within Russia. This form of communication is also frequently used for military purposes at tactical level, given the inadequacy of the service equipment. This situation is frequently used to their advantage by Ukrainian units, being able to listen to tactical instructions issued to Russian units, and act accordingly. This story is a virtually verbatim one-way conversation between a soldier and his mother, living in the town of Kizhinga in the federal district of Buryatia.

> Dear Mamma, I hope that you are well and the rest of the family also. Thank you for your food parcel. The food given to us here is generally very poor, often tinned vegetables and semi-mouldy bread. I and my fellow platoon members are now in Severodonetsk, allegedly on peacekeeping duty. There is not much left of the city to keep peace in as our artillery shelled it for about three weeks before the Ukrainians moved out and we took over the rubble. Mamma, I do not understand what we are doing here. When we crossed the border from Russia, we were told that we were here to protect the local population from fascists. I do not know who they are. All the local people I have met swear at us and shake their fists. This is not surprising given the state to which we have reduced their city. My platoon lives in the cellar of a bombed block of flats. There is no electricity, water or sanitary system. Where do the locals now live? What have we done? What did the Ukrainians do to deserve this punishment? They can speak our language, but I prefer not to hear what they have to say. We go out as a group occasionally as there are some cafés open on the edges of the city, outside the main area of destruction. We try to meet locals and buy a coffee or a beer, but not one will talk with us. This makes us feel very lonely. The only contact with local people is when they hold rallies against our presence, and then we have to behave brutally to maintain order. Sometimes, we have to use tear gas and fire our rifles over their heads. At night, we only go out in groups.

We are fearful of the people we meet: we have lost two of our platoon, who seem to have died accidentally. All of us hate this place. All of my platoon members come from Buryatia. Our officers are from western Russia, but most of the soldiers I meet are from Siberia. The story going round is that the Kremlin wants to limit the number of dead soldiers returned to their homes in Moscow or St Petersburg and prefer that news of the large numbers of casualties is told only in Siberia. Mamma, I do not like it here and would like to come home. The sooner this terrible war and all the death and destruction it causes is over, the better. I love Russia but not this Russia.

A footnote from our correspondent

I have removed the distressing comments and prayers for his safety which Kozlov's mother made during the course of the phone call. She was understandably very upset.

CHAPTER THREE

The War Goes On

Discussion of Russia's weakening relationship with China and mention of the Aigun Treaty.

The War Goes On

The Historical Relationship between Russia and China

Extracts from a Paper by China Forward on Siberia

The War Goes On

A paper published in London by New Europe – A London-based think tank

The President of Russia's unprovoked invasion of Ukraine has created a new and destabilising geopolitical situation in Europe. The relatively routine stability of the continent has been overturned. The President's desire to recreate the geographical and political boundaries of the Soviet Union has reawakened fears of instability in the original constituent countries of what is now regarded as eastern Europe. He has also created great unease in EU countries suddenly confronted with the old enemy, which was thought to be at rest. The Russian Federation has only a small portion of the economic and military strength of the Soviets. Its very poor performance in its war in Ukraine, against a much smaller power, has shown it to be a much- diminished power compared with the superpower status still conferred on it by the West. Any critical examination of Russia's economic, financial and military capability indicates that, even if it tried, it would not be capable of regaining even a small part of the old Soviet Empire. However, it still has the natural resources, especially oil and gas, to use as a form of blackmail against the unprepared and soft democratic states of the EU. The President has enough power to bully his way to a position of strength if the EU, combined with NATO, allows it. What is more, he appears to have the fanaticism and boldness to try. The EU/NATO has to project the strength it already has, against which his endeavours will fail. The danger to EU/NATO is the extent to which the many nations comprising both organisations are firm in deciding on and sticking to their aim, which must be to defeat the Russian President's adventurism, and hold on to that aim despite any setbacks and problems which he will create to try to break their steadfastness.

There has been much discussion of the President's possible frail health and/or insurrection amongst his peers, but it cannot be left to chance that either will eventually make the threat go away. A truce has to be declared. He may regard this as a victory, but any pause will be short-lived, and the Russian President's renewal of his war to achieve his declared long-term aim can be expected. The implications of the terms of any truce will be examined in a later paper. We are also concerned about the involvement of China, having aligned itself with Russia as closely as it seems. China's motives are likely to be less obvious than is apparent. We will also present our views of the Russia/China relationship and how each country hopes to benefit, in a later paper.

Historical Record

The Relationship between Russia and China

A paper published by New Europe:

A manifestation of national confidence by the new Chinese Republic, established in 1912, was demonstrated by the despatch in 1917 of troops to support White Russian opponents of the Soviet Revolution in 1917. White Russian forces were soon overcome and Soviets showed their confidence by creating a pro-Soviet communist regime in the form of the Mongolian People's Republic. This display of the Soviet Union's support for the spread of communism did not prevent it, in the 1920s, from supporting in its own interests the right-wing Kuomintang Government of China (KMT) and advising the fledgling Chinese communist movement, the CCP, to support it. This cooperation did not last and the KMT and CCP went to war in 1927. The civil war ended in 1950 with the defeat of the KMT, its army retreating to and taking over the island of Taiwan. The triumphant CCP, led by Mao Zedong, had earlier proclaimed the new People's Republic of China, the PRC. The Soviet Union had by now abandoned the KMT and provided support to the PRC. This was particularly the case after a Soviet army marched into Manchuria in 1945. The Japanese Empire had invaded Manchuria in

1931, establishing the puppet state of Manchukuo. The occupying Japanese Army was defeated by the Soviet Army. The Soviet Union continued to support the PRC between 1945 and 1950, by which time, Russia and China were controlled by amicable communist parties with the same Marxist-Leninist ideology. Amity continued for a number of years, with Russia providing significant economic, technical and military support to help with the industrialisation of the PRC. However, the separate strands of communism began to separate ideologically, with Russia moving away from original communist ideology whilst China preferred staying with its Stalinist principles. The ideological split was reflected in international communist beliefs and behaviour. This was illustrated in their different attitudes towards India. Russia regarded India as a strategic partner and major customer for Soviet military equipment, whilst China regarded India as a potential rival and initiated minor military forays on India's northern border. A fierce ideological split developed between China and Russia, which withdrew the support it had previously offered. These differences were emphasised by the Mao Zedong-inspired Cultural Revolution and were reflected in the heavy militarisation of the border between the two countries. This led to an extended series of military confrontations along the Ussuri River border between 1969 and 1980. The two countries were engaged in a minor war. There was some reconciliation following Mao's death, but the ideological differences were re-emphasised by the abrupt change brought about by the dissolution of the Soviet Union. The Soviet system was chaotically overthrown, from 1989, principally under the government controlled by Boris Yeltsin, in a series of mismanaged privatisations. These did not lead to an efficient industrial economy which relied instead on the extraction and export of hydrocarbons to provide the main portion of the state income. In the coming years, Russian technological and service provision was to develop at a pedestrian rate. China, however, starting in 1976 under the leadership of Deng Xiaoping, showed remarkable initiative in copying and emulating the industries of the West and rapidly achieved economic development in all major sectors, which doubled and trebled the rate achieved by Russia. From a position of very approximately parity in economic output in the 1970s, China rapidly became a behemoth in relation to Russia's pigmy. It is likely that Russia's invasion of Ukraine in 2022 will eventually cause so much economic damage that the gap in the GDP outputs of the two countries is likely to be significantly widened.

The difference is shown in the International Monetary Fund (IMF) forecast of GDP for 2022 for nations of interest shown below (In US Dollars):

USA	25,000 million
CHINA	20,000 million
RUSSIA	1,800 million
UK	3,300 million
S. KOREA	1,800 million
AUSTRALIA	1,800 million

Russia is now seen as an economic minnow: a rogue state and a superpower only in that it possesses a large nuclear arsenal, acquired on the demise of the Soviet Union. Its economy is hardly able to sustain its internal social requirements and certainly not able, in the long term, to sustain its overlarge military posture. Russia and China started the twentieth century as approximate equals and initially continued to display communist-derived agreement. That position has changed radically: both countries are now in ideological agreement only to the extent that both are outward-looking, thuggish centralised powers whose main aim is to maintain their power whilst aggressively attempting to extend their empires. Their only shared international position is one of hostility towards the USA. This does not change their relative status as minnow and behemoth.

Extracts from a paper by China forward on Siberia

From our Correspondent in Beijing

This paper addresses the situation arising from what we now see as the fragility of China's de facto western border, that is, Russia's western border with NATO. The territorial gap between that border and China's northern border is Siberia, all of it controlled by Russia and therefore a part of China's western border. China needs to extend its northern border westwards to create a strategic buffer zone between it and any encroachment from the West, for instance by NATO.

This paper raises our view that the time has come for China to renegotiate the terms of the 1858 Treaty of Aigun, and recover the northern territory lost under the terms of that treaty. We are concerned by the poor military capability displayed by Russia in its war with Ukraine. Russia's population is 10% of China's, as is its GDP. By inflicting a reduced quality of life on its population and by reducing its investment in infrastructure, research and development, Russia continues to field armed forces of over one million personnel (still only 50% of China's strength). However, the poor performance of Russia's military in Ukraine, against a much smaller force, raises significant doubts about its real capability. Despite spending estimated at more than 20% of its limited GDP on defence, it is proving to be a paper tiger. Russia can design and produce very capable weapon systems but does not have the economic and manufacturing resources to equip its armed forces as it would like. Displaying sophisticated and boastful capabilities in Red Square parades does not make up for the fact that the bulk of its military is more likely to be equipped with increasingly outdated material. Its army appears to be short of logistic capability, modern artillery and armoured vehicles. Soldiers, mainly conscripts, appear to be ill trained and lack leadership in the lower ranks. Soldiers have poor individual skills. The command structure demonstrates a lack of flexibility and an all-arms operating capability. Russia's displayed capability leaves little doubt that it could not compete with NATO or China's military should either deploy it. Russia has to secure its southern borders including those with Turkey, Kazakhstan, Mongolia and, of course, China itself. Given its economic and military capability, its borders are, by any rational reasoning, indefensible. In theory, China could assist in defending those borders but in China's national interest? Indeed, we have argued that a significant part of the existing Russia/China border should, in any case, revert to Chinese control. The current regime in Russia will surely fall. What replaces it is open to conjecture, but it is certainly possible that a regime more democratically inclined would find favour in western Europe and a slow process of integration of Russia into western Europe could follow. Possible outcomes of this process could be the acceptance of Russia into the EU and even into NATO. Either or both of these events could have very significant consequences for China. Russia will become progressively economically and militarily weaker as time goes by. It could well regard linkage to western Europe as the only sure way of protecting its Siberian Empire. Clause 5 of the NATO treaty states that all treaty countries will be protected, by military force if necessary, should they suffer attack. It is perfectly feasible that, at some time in the future, NATO forces could be welcomed into Russia, and by implication, into the whole of Siberia. It will not be in China's interests for European military forces to be located in Russia's Far East. This would be hugely detrimental to China's strategic interests and cannot be allowed to happen. Even the remote possibility of it happening should become China's priority strategic interest. China must short circuit this possibility by moving first and recovering the whole of Far East Siberia as soon as possible. It must not wait for events to unfold in its disfavour. It is for the Chinese Government to discuss and decide on the implications of the existence of Russia's nuclear arsenal, which, at over 5,000 warheads, is significantly greater than the 1,000 plus, possessed by China. The long-established doctrine of avoidance of nuclear war by the assurance of 'mutual self-destruction' could come into play. However, it would be prudent of China to consider delaying any action in Siberia until its own nuclear arsenal adequately matches Russia's with first-and second-strike capability. This is a political decision. Timing will depend on the interpretation of any increase in potential threat arising in the West. It will also be heavily dependent on the assessment of the capability of Russia's nuclear force to deter China, and an assessment of the capability of China's increasingly effective nuclear arsenal to deter any action by Russia. This is a major decision for the Chinese Government to take, at the appropriate time.

CHAPTER FOUR

Chinese and NATO Comments on the War

China Forward expresses concern about Russia's poor military achievements and NATO warns Russia to desist from continuing attacks on Ukrainian infrastructure or face military consequences.

China's rising concern about Russia's reliability

EU/NATO response to Russian aggression

The ongoing bombardment of Ukraine

Russia's response to the NATO statement

China's rising concern about Russia's reliability

A paper by China Forward

The President of China and the President of the Russian Federation met in Beijing in February 2022. No new treaty relationship was established but both leaders made statements extolling their long and continuing relationship and emphasised that the relationship was being re-established for the long term.

For China, partnership with Russia provided backing for its ongoing and disputatious relationship with the United States of America. This involved a widening rift in the conduct of economic affairs, the USA having imposed trade sanctions on China and strict limitations on technical trade and information transfer. Their geopolitical relationship centres on China's claim to sovereignty over a large part of the South China Sea and, in particular, over the sovereignty of Taiwan: the USA has come close to saying that it would provide military support to Taiwan in the event of an invasion by China. China recognises that its growing economic and military power begins to approach that of the USA, but it also recognises the continuing superiority of the USA, given their relative military power deployed across the world.

For Russia, the meeting and the declaration of mutual interests provided the equivalent of superpower backing to add to its own diminished capability, especially in its undeclared intention to invade Ukraine. There is no public record of any discussion on this topic, but it has to be assumed that such a discussion took place and that at least tacit approval to the invasion was given by the President of China. This approval did not extend to public approval or promise of help. As the war in Ukraine has progressed, the absence of such a promise has been shown by the lack of any significant support.

China Forward is now concerned at the situation in Ukraine revealed by Russia's inability to subdue the Ukrainian Army. Russia purports to have achieved its main invasion aim by occupying the Donbas, whilst ignoring its main original aim of occupying Kyiv, installing a president more pliant to Russia's wishes. By his actions, the Russian President has worsened significantly his country's geopolitical position: Sweden and Finland are joining NATO, whilst the embittered population of Ukraine is further than ever from being a cooperative neighbour to Russia. Russia has created for itself a new and geographically extended hostile border to its west. China Forward is concerned about the implications of this new situation on China's strategic safety.

Russia has shown itself to be inferior militarily to NATO. The latter is genuinely concerned only in protecting the geographic integrity of its constituent nations. But this concern could well spill over to side issues affecting the well-being of those nations. Cutting off gas and oil supplies to western nations and consequently taking military action by either side to protect their supplies could arguably be included in this category. This is an unlikely possibility, but its very existence emphasises the potential fragility of China's western border, in theory protected by Russia and its Siberian land mass.

China Forward believes that the faith placed in the protection of China's western strategic border by Russia is now questionable. Russia's activities in Ukraine have weakened it economically, financially and militarily. Starting from a low base capability, it must be questionable as to how Russia will be capable of restoring itself to the low capability it possessed prior to its Ukraine adventure.

China's western flank is now far less secure than has been assumed prior to this date. This strategic deficit must now be addressed. China Forward will discuss this in a subsequent paper.

EU/NATO response to Russian aggression

A statement made by the Secretary General of NATO

I wish to brief you on the discussions held between the assembled foreign ministers of coalition countries. They have discussed the actions considered necessary to deal with Russia's threat of renewed aggression. The first point is to mention that Russia has now abandoned its cover story of 'Special Military Operation' in Ukraine and has declared through the Duma that Russia is now at war with Ukraine. This declaration means that the government can put the whole country into a state of martial law and can deploy additional financial, manufacturing and human resources to enhance its combat capability. A theoretical total of more or less one million additional reservists could be added to Russia's order of battle. In practice, the very low standard of training which these men have undergone, and the relatively small stockpile of old and frequently unserviceable equipment available, very much lowers the utility of the additional soldiers. Nevertheless, as individuals, they can be used in the traditional tactic of mass attack, without concern about casualty levels and as individual replacements of casualties in line units.

A fundamental principle agreed by all attending is that a continuation of massive damage to infrastructure and, consequently, very significant military and civilian casualties in Ukraine can no longer be tolerated. Any further aggression must be halted using maximum force, and as quickly as possible with whatever force is required, and this must be made clear to Russia. This action will also apply to any aggression launched from Russian territory.

Threats to resort to nuclear weapons have been made on a number of occasions by the President of Russia. Use of low-yield tactical nuclear weapons on the battlefield is part of routine Russian battlefield doctrine. Low-yield weapons launched by air or battlefield launchers are capable of destroying men and equipment within a radius of at least two kilometres. The President is in a position to authorise such activity. The Russian high command system will have a controlling function prior to launch, but it should be assumed that their actual use would be authorised, if necessary, by the Russian high command. The Russian President has issued threats frequently to the extent that his threats seem rather hollow, but they remain a possibility, including the risk of escalation to higher yield levels. Nevertheless, we have collectively resolved to inform Russia that NATO also has a nuclear battlefield capability which will be used in response to any first use of such weapons by Russia. This intent has been formally stated by NATO headquarters to the Russian General Staff.

I wish to update you on the provision of equipment and ammunition to Ukraine's armed forces. You have already been briefed on our force deployments but I now update you as follows:

We have a total of one hundred and twenty thousand personnel in armoured formations in the Baltic states, another armoured brigade guarding the Sulalki Gap, over one hundred and forty thousand, primarily US Marines, in Poland and about twenty thousand personnel around Kyiv, controlling economic, military and training aid to Ukraine: a total approaching three hundred thousand soldiers with appropriate equipment. We have now supplied over two hundred self-propelled and towed artillery pieces of 155mm calibre, with enough ammunition for an estimated four months of usage, seven hundred and fifty armoured personnel carriers, three hundred and fifty tanks, mainly T72s, provided by countries previously part of the Warsaw Pact, who have received in exchange an equal number of NATO standard tanks. Seventy-five Russian Mig fighters have been provided, again by previous Warsaw Pact countries, who have received F16s in return, and another seventy-five bought commercially from countries around the world. A wide range of other artillery and support vehicles have also been provided. All in all, Ukraine's military is now well equipped and in a much stronger position than it has been seen since the start of this conflict.

This information is published as encouragement to all our NATO and allied forces and as a positive sign of our intent to Russia, which should dissuade it from any further military adventures, in particular, against any NATO country.

I end by saying that NATO have not declared a state of hostilities with Russia but that condition will exist as a consequence of any hostile move by Russia in which NATO forces suffer any casualties or damage as a result of such action.

The ongoing bombardment of Ukraine

A statement by the Secretary General of NATO in a press release

The NATO council has met to discuss the ongoing bombardment of Ukraine by Russian guided and unguided missiles. The death of civilians and damage to civilian infrastructure is being caused on a daily basis. Any pretence that Russia's war is intended to save the population from a fascist regime has been totally abandoned. NATO is not prepared to allow this bombardment to continue indefinitely. Russia must understand that NATO will prevent any further death and destruction by the installation of anti-missile systems manned, if necessary, by NATO forces. In addition to the destruction of incoming missiles, NATO will now also attack the launch sites wherever they are situated, be they in Ukraine, on ships at sea, within Russian territory, or aircraft delivered. If this position cannot be achieved by ground-based weapons, then NATO will provide air cover to ensure achievement.

We have been able to agree to Ukraine's request for F16s to be provided to their air force, and we are now providing air defence cover by deploying NATO aircraft, as I have described, if necessary. NATO aircraft will not operate outside Ukrainian territory but will be equipped with missiles with sufficient range to attack targets within Russia if necessary. Our aircraft will not be used in support of Ukrainian ground activities. I emphasise this position in order to minimise the extent of our initiative, whose primary purpose is to stop the ongoing destruction of Ukrainian infrastructure and civilian deaths at the present time and into the future.

Russia is forcing this position on us by its constant offensive action against civilian targets. NATO action increases the risk of direct Russian/NATO conflict and we ask that Russia de-escalate its activities and thus prevent the clash we wish to avoid.

Russia's response to the NATO statement

A statement issued by Russia's Foreign Secretary on Ukraine

We are close to achieving our military objective in Ukraine. All the targets which we have attacked to date have been military. We have not targeted any civilian buildings. We believe that the Ukrainian military have frequently targeted their own population and blamed it on Russian forces to try to achieve some propaganda success. Irrespective of the NATO announcement, we will therefore continue to attack military targets and avoid civilian collateral damage as far as possible. We expect the Ukrainian military to behave in the same way and cease blaming Russian forces for the damage the Ukrainians have caused. The NATO announcement has therefore no effect on our battle plans. It also needs to be said that any attack on Russian land, air or naval forces by NATO will be regarded as an act of war, and will be met by a forceful response.

Comments by our defence correspondent

NATO's announcement is timely in that there is evidence that Russia is close to exhausting its stock of guided munitions and is having difficulty in restocking, partly because of the limitations on its manufacturing capacity and also because of the effect of sanctions on the supply of essential components normally imported into Russia. The same is partly true in respect of unguided missiles launched by artillery or air dropped. Russia would risk a head-on conflict with NATO forces if missiles continue to be used. Experience will tell of the extent to which such munitions are used and the level of consequent counterforce strikes by NATO forces.

CHAPTER FIVE

A Short-Lived Truce

Russian and Ukrainian armies are exhausted. A truce is arranged but quickly broken by Russia. NATO responds with air attacks in the Donbas, within Russia and on the Black Sea Fleet.

The first ceasefire: Russia and Ukraine

By New Europe

Hostilities between Ukraine and Russia lost much of their momentum as both sides exhausted themselves and sought a truce/ceasefire. By this time, Russia had occupied much of the Donbas area and the Russian President was prepared to announce to the Russian public that the aims of the 'Special Military Operation' had been achieved. The Russian public had never in fact been briefed as to what these aims were and were collectively more than pleased to hear that fighting had ceased. In fact, Russia had achieved relatively very little: an extension of the already occupied area of Donbas, extension of that area to connect it to Crimea, and an extension towards Kherson which the Ukrainians had lost and then recovered. Odesa and Kyiv remained out of Russia's reach.

To achieve this limited gain, Russia had lost a thousand tanks, one thousand six hundred other armoured vehicles, forty strike aircraft and over thirty thousand soldiers killed, with four times that many injured. It had also lost a cruiser and two frigates plus other minor naval vessels in the Black Sea. Its economy, as a consequence of sanctions, had shrunk by 5% with continuing reduction into the foreseeable future. The living standards of its people were being driven down. The President of Russia's boast of victory was ill-matched to the result. Russia's armed forces committed to the Ukrainian War were exhausted. A ceasefire was forced on it. What was uncertain to Ukraine and allied Western forces was whether a ceasefire was regarded by Russia as temporary, whilst it reorganised itself, or whether it signified a change of heart and direction. Widespread opinion regarded the former as more likely. For its part, Ukraine had suffered grievously as a consequence of the unprovoked invasion. It had lost at least a third of the military capability it had at the start of the invasion. This had been partly made up from western allies by the provision of new and better equipment, but training on the wide range of new unfamiliar equipment had become a problem, and time to recruit, train and reorganise was welcome. Much of the social, industrial and urban infrastructure in the battlefield area had been destroyed, and indiscriminate missile attacks had also caused much damage to infrastructure elsewhere. The reconstruction cost of this damage was estimated at about five hundred billion US dollars. Ukraine's population had, at least temporarily, lost about five million refugees, who had moved to friendly countries. It was anticipated that a large proportion would move back once peace was established. Ukraine now required support from its western allies to rebuild its military, to meet routine outlays on wages and other government expenditure, and provide general support to a very damaged population. The annual funding required to support these activities was assessed as thirty billion US dollars per year. It is expected by Ukraine's allies that a significant proportion of these funds will be extracted from Russian government funds held overseas and from taxes on Russian oil and gas production. It was expected that a ceasefire would not run smoothly. Ukraine partisans in occupied territory would constantly cause problems to the Russian occupiers. Russia would continue to deny Ukraine access to its Black Sea ports and would be expected to cause trouble wherever possible. Ukraine could start rebuilding itself but western allies would have to continue to support it, militarily and economically, for some years to come. The EU and NATO also had to readdress their commitments to the Baltic states, Georgia and Moldova, and be ready for a probable reawakening by the Russian President of his declared desire to recreate its imperial and Soviet empires by absorbing those states. This high level of uncertainty about Russia's diminished status, and of its continuing ambitions for imperial grandeur, was giving China cause for concern that its new-found friend protecting its northern border had become unstable.

Ukraine: Situation post-hostilities

By our Defence Editor

The conflict between Ukraine and Russia continued to the point where both sides achieved the maximum gains they were likely to achieve in the short term. Russia had lost Kharkiv and Kherson and made no further gains in Donbas, whilst Ukraine had lost Severodonetsk and did not recover the major part of Luhansk already lost. The Russian President proclaimed to the Russian public that he had won by gaining Luhansk, consolidating his grip on Donetsk and gaining Mariupol and further territory to the west of Crimea. Desultory negotiations were thus held. Ukraine, whilst currently not being able to recover any further territory, was not prepared to accept the long-term loss of land seized by Russia. France, representing the EU and as a member of the Security Council, therefore proposed the establishment of a UN peacekeeping force to prevent further hostilities. This was, unsurprisingly, vetoed by Russia. At this point, the remaining members of the Security Council, supported by the General Secretary of the UN, proposed that the issue be referred to the full UN Assembly. An Assembly vote was held at which China and India abstained but the vote was otherwise unanimous: a truce was to be called and monitored. The Secretary General Secretariat assumed responsibility for the formation of the peacekeeping force. France was accepted as the lead nation and sponsored NATO as the headquarters. Japan and South Korea immediately volunteered to provide contingents, as did a number of Asian and African countries. NATO had troops close at hand and the peacekeeping force was established within days, with headquarters at Kyiv. The only country to recognise the self-proclaimed Republics of Luhansk and Donetsk was Belarus. Both republics, whilst having a significant Russian population, were to prove restive, with acts of minor sabotage and civil unrest continuing. The civil and military unrest and the existence of Ukraine's military forces on their borders forced Russia to maintain a large military force within their borders, in order to maintain control.

Truce-keeping force

Our Correspondent at Truce Headquarters, Kyiv

Russia and Ukraine required the temporary cessation of hostilities to be called a truce and not a ceasefire. The truce-keeping force was commanded by a French general, with staff providing him with personal protection and sufficient manpower to allow liaison with Ukraine and Russian governments, NATO HQ and the UN Secretariat. It was based in Kyiv.

NATO provided all communication equipment, soft-skinned vehicles for use by deployed patrols and all the logistical and personal support required by patrolling personnel. They carried their own small arms which were to be used strictly for self-defence. In the event of encountering any form of hostility, they were instructed to withdraw and rejoin their units. These units consisted of the equivalent of five battalions located so as to allow patrols to cover the effective front lines, reaching from Kharkiv in the east to Kherson in the west. Two thousand personnel came from the countries of Japan, South Korea and Mongolia. The combatants' front line positions were fully manned and in depth, prepared for any attack their prospective enemy could launch.

The first few days of the truce were calm, with no hostile artillery, small arms or personnel movement detected. Both sides were content to put all their efforts into reorganising and re-equipping their forces. A resumption of hostilities was regarded as inevitable. Patrol reports were strictly concerned with activities on the front lines, but many reported that the Russian-controlled areas seemed fairly lively. Small arms fire, mostly single shots but with occasional bursts of fire suggesting minor engagements, occurred frequently. Civilians escaping from the Donbas area to the Ukrainian side reported activity mostly at night, with small groups or individual Russian soldiers being ambushed or killed. Numerous Russian vehicles parked overnight burst into flames when they moved the following day, having had mines placed beneath them. Partisan groups appeared to be operating and in possession of explosives, hence the destruction of vehicles and building fires caused by explosive charges thrown through windows. The Russian occupation was not being allowed to continue smoothly. Numerous Russian patrols failed in their efforts to prevent high-level disorder. Russian forces were forced to deploy large numbers of soldiers to guard military facilities. This level of engagement did not bode well for their plan of holding on to the urban areas they had overrun, or for their plans to withdraw units to reinforce their army in eastern Siberia, if this became necessary.

A briefing by the NATO Secretary General on Ultimate Peace Treaty Terms

Attended by our Defence Correspondent

I speak for the EU and NATO.

The President of Russia invaded Ukraine without any legitimate reason. He massed troops on their mutual border but consistently denied that he intended to invade. He lied. He claimed that his 'Special Military Operation' was designed to rid Ukraine of its Nazis whilst also claiming that he would protect the peoples of the Donbas area from the alleged genocidal actions of the Ukraine Government. He also uttered a constant refrain that Ukraine should not exist as it was properly part of Russia. He expressed an ambition to restore Russia to its imperial past. His aim clearly involved restoring lands previously part of that imperial past to what he regarded as their rightful place. That is, within Russia. This ambition was of great concern to other countries bordering Ukraine, in particular Poland and the Baltic states: close neighbours. These countries are members of the EU and NATO. This position created the potential for a military clash.

Our joint response represents the will of all the peoples of Europe and the overwhelming majority of democratic countries outside Europe and North America. It was a major strategic error by the Russian President to have failed to recognise the international political consequences of his action. Ukraine's aim is to recover all the territory lost to Russia, including that lost in February 2014, including Crimea. This long-term aim is supported. The extent to which it is achieved will depend on the extent to which Ukraine is adequately supported by EU and NATO, and by Ukraine's own wishes. At some stage, a treaty will need to be negotiated between Ukraine and Russia. The main aim of this briefing is to outline the position of EU/NATO in advising on the terms of the treaty and participating in its implementation.

The President of Russia lied his way into this war and cannot be trusted not to repeat his actions at a future date unless the penalties for doing so are too great for Russia to bear. The major elements of such a treaty will be assured by EU/NATO as guarantors. These should include:

1. The boundaries of the Ukraine state will be agreed by international law and will not be violated under any circumstances by Russia, or any other state. Sanctions will follow violation of this or any other transgression. These borders will replicate those existing prior to February 2014.

2. Ukrainian air space will be honoured. Any intrusion not agreed by Ukraine will be met by armed response provided by NATO aircraft, maintaining a 'no-fly zone' over Ukraine.

3. Bombardment of any sort targeting Ukraine territory will be met by air strikes or any other appropriate military action directed at the source of the bombardment. This response will apply should the source be within Russia or its Black Sea fleet or any territory acting on its behalf.

4. Any form of IT interference, including hacking, of Ukrainian public or private IT network will be met by overwhelming physical and/or digital attack of the IT source.

5. Ukraine has applied to join the EU and accepts the conditions which have to be met to achieve eventual confirmation of membership. Any attack on organisations or facilities intended to assist in the achievement of this goal will attract like countermeasures and sanctions.

6. Ukraine will need to rebuild its armed forces. This will be aided by NATO, including the stationing of any training force required, together with necessary military protection, as mutually agreed with Ukraine.

7. Ukraine has expressed a desire to join NATO. All NATO members have joined by their free will and Ukraine's membership will be assessed on that basis once joining parameters have been met. In principle, its potential membership has already been found acceptable by existing members.

8. A coordinating headquarters already functions to assess Ukraine's ongoing battlefield and long-term equipment requirements to

achieve longer-term army, navy and airforce goals. Ukraine will need funds to achieve its buying programme. This will be discussed with EU/NATO but the aim will be to achieve modern tri-service forces up to NATO standards as quickly as possible.

9. I have stated that the President of Russia cannot be trusted to refrain from further aggression. The EU and NATO now formally state that, following any treaty agreed between Ukraine and Russia, and before the signing of a formal agreement, NATO will regard any aggression against Ukraine by Russia as an attack on a Member State and will apply whatever military means are required, involving NATO armed forces, to repel that aggression. This intent already applies to existing NATO members and Russia may need to be reminded of this, in particular in respect of the Baltic states and Poland. It also needs to be stated that Finland and Sweden have applied to join NATO. The Russian President has made belligerent statements in respect of those states. They must now be regarded as being already protected by the NATO umbrella, as already described above.

10. Odesa: Russia has now agreed to shipments of grain to leave Odesa. This agreement must apply to any future shipping requirements. NATO will enforce this process if necessary.

11. Reparations: The use of massed artillery, missiles and airpower has laid waste to large areas of Ukraine, particularly in the east and south. The material damage by this onslaught has been assessed, to date, at a minimum of five hundred billion US dollars. The output lost as a result of this damage will add hundreds of millions to this total. When his initial military assault failed, the President of Russia set out to create as much damage to Ukraine as possible. He must now pay for it by an initial payment and ongoing reparations. A proposal to confiscate Russia's holdings of overseas currency held in western banks, as a down payment, is supported. Further payments will need to be made and must form an integral principle in the final agreement reached between Russia and Ukraine.

It is conceivable that Ukraine and Russia may not be able to agree a treaty leading to cessation of armed conflict. In this event, EU/NATO will seek to create the conditions and guarantees which would have followed the negotiations of such a treaty. This will be done through the UN by seeking the approval of the General Assembly to condemn any aggression by Russia and by giving approval to the establishment of a peacekeeping force. NATO would accept responsibility to lead this force and contribute to it but would, through the UN, call for other nations to join it.

At the beginning of this statement, I noted that the Russian President had made a significant strategic error in assuming that the EU and NATO would not react strongly to his aggression. I assume that he is now disabused and that no further acts of aggression will be contemplated. Force will be applied to resist him should he commit such acts.

The effect of the invasion on the Russian/Chinese détente

A paper by the China Forward think tank

We have already issued a paper on the detailed consequences of the Russian President's bizarre and disastrous invasion of Ukraine on the social, economic and military condition of Russia. All these areas have been significantly damaged. In 2022, the Russian President and the Chinese President very publicly announced a pact that bound them together as blood brothers for the foreseeable future. The President of Russia saw this as a backstop of support for his forthcoming Ukrainian invasion: his 'Special Military Operation'. The President of China saw it as a major addition to his bargaining power vis-à-vis his increasingly bellicose confrontation with the USA. China now sees Russian inadequacies revealed by an underwhelming performance against a smaller and theoretically much weaker state and thus sees Russia as a very much weaker supporting state than had been assumed. Russia's people have been hoodwinked into supporting an unsupportable war. Their standard of living has been diminished, and Russia's military, having suffered grievous losses, has become less capable of defending its own territory. Moreover, the sanctions forced on Russia by the western powers and the very large reduction of hydrocarbon revenue have so lowered its financial stability that it will take some time to recover, if ever it is able. China's pact with Russia has become much less relevant to China's security and it must now think again about its strategic position.

This paper points out the dangers that confront China and re-emphasises its previous advice on dealing with Siberia. This paper now makes the assumption, given Russia's weakened position, that it has become incapable of defending its position as hegemonic and military protector of

Siberia. The strategic dangers that confront it will be examined. Essentially, these lie in its north-eastern territory and also its western border with NATO. It is highly unlikely that NATO has any intention of breaching borders, but the possibility creates a strategic situation which China could find at least uncomfortable, and in the long term, possibly dangerous. These geopolitical and geographic weaknesses should be addressed. This paper will examine them.

Russian territory stretches northwards from its eastern provinces to the Bering Straits, where it borders the USA state of Alaska, across a narrow sea. Alaska has a population of about eight hundred thousand and in its cold war confrontation with Russia (from whom the USA bought the state in 1867 for the sum of seven million dollars), the USA has always been prepared to defend its territory. It has a current military population of about sixty thousand personnel. It has seven army bases and two air force bases. Military forces include at least one infantry division with supporting arms and services and a fleet of aircraft in the 11th Group Air Force. All the military are part of US Pacific Command. The defence strategy includes missile early warning, missile defence systems and radar covering Russian Siberia. It joins Canada in the North America Air Defence Command, NORAD, and exercises its air force regularly with Canadian and UK air forces. There are no naval bases in Alaska but the US Pacific Fleet is close at hand. This display of military power has historically been a potential threat to Russian Siberia and continues to be so. Should China ever replace Russia in eastern Siberia, it has to be aware of the existing presence of the USA.

Japan also poses a potential threat to China in eastern Siberia. Japan has a long- running dispute with Russia over the Kuril Islands and over the Island of Sakhalin. The latter was historically shared by Russia and Japan until Russia's very late entry into the Second World War, when it defeated the local Japanese army and took control of the entire island. At the same time, it occupied the Kuril Islands and has remained there ever since. It is assumed that China would not engage Japan in hostilities over these islands, but Japan's historic claims would have to be respected in any confrontation in East Siberia.

The President of Russia's prime aim in invading Ukraine, apart from the cover story provided by the declared need to rid Ukraine of its alleged fascist government and absorb the country into Imperial Russia, was to push NATO further away from its western border. The reverse appears to have been achieved, in that Russia is likely to have a new and extended border, created by Finland joining NATO. It has also turned Ukraine from a country which was not intending to join NATO and a country with whom collaboration would have worked perfectly well, to a bitter enemy now programmed to join the EU and probably, in due course, to join NATO also.

The next major problem for the Russian President will be the survival, in its present form, of the government of Belarus, which borders on Poland, the Baltic states, Ukraine and Russia. In 2020, mock elections were held which led to the President of Belarus being elected, to Russian acclaim, to a sixth term in office. The defeated popular choice, the Opposition leader in Belarus, just avoided arrest and fled to the Baltic states. Mass demonstrations were put down with brutality, aided by two thousand Russian soldiers. The President of Belarus' governing cohort are entirely dependent on Russia and its president for survival. Given the depth of public hostility, the regime could easily collapse into a democratic government, wishing to achieve membership of the EU and NATO. The final problem for Russia is on its south-western border, where it needs to maintain the loyalty of Ingushetia, Dagestan and Chechnya with their Muslim populations. All three currently require Russian political pressure and occasional use of force to maintain control over hostile populations. Enmity towards Georgia and uneasy relations with Azerbaijan complete the package of troublesome neighbours. Sitting in the wings will always be Turkey, conscious of the fact that the South Caucasus was historically part of the Ottoman Empire.

Any collapse of Russian control over these areas could invite intervention from western Europe, creating a potential problem for China. A longer-term view of this situation would see Russia beset with all these problems and, as a consequence of its inevitable decline, rediscovering its roots and becoming a fully joined-up member of the European family. This could imply that the EU would have a political influence in the governance of Siberia and become the northern neighbour of China. NATO is not formally linked to the EU but the link is very strong, and NATO could well emerge in some form in Siberia. This situation would not be acceptable to China. The geopolitical situation needs to be resolved by China before these circumstances arise.

In an earlier paper, we raised the possibility of China assisting Russia in this war in Ukraine. Such assistance would possibly stabilise Russia's borders and therefore protect China's. Given Russia's dismal performance in Ukraine and the very major loss of equipment, especially armour, it is quite likely that Russia has already sought material assistance from China. To date, this assistance has not been provided. China must consider its options, including the possibility that Russia could lose its war in Ukraine and be driven back to its own borders. In that event, NATO forces could end up along Russia's borders, from the Baltic to the Black Sea. Options available to China in this event will be discussed in a later paper.

Implementation of the ceasefire

By our Correspondent in Kyiv

The Russians had not wanted a total ceasefire, although, given the heavy losses they had sustained, a ceasefire would have been an opportunity for them to regroup their battered units and continue their offensive. They would have preferred a slowing of operations and not the loss of momentum that a ceasefire brought about. They also regarded a ceasefire imposed by the UN as a loss of face. The Ukrainian Government accepted the terms of the cessation of hostility and it put a least a temporary stay on its strongly felt need to recover territory lost to Russia. The Ukrainian Government also had some concern that the UN, and even their western allies and backers, could regard the situation with relief and reason to pause their efforts to sustain Ukraine. Providing Ukraine with weapons systems and ammunition was creating some problems for NATO countries, which had become accustomed to low stock levels. Minimum numbers of weapon systems and ammunition stocks were retained for their own forces, and material already provided to Ukraine represented a significant proportion of what they regarded as minimum stocks. There would be a delay whilst replenishment factories, especially where vehicles and equipment were concerned, geared up production to make up for Ukraine's high levels of consumption whilst maintaining NATO countries' inventories at a level adequate to meet any wider conflict which Russia could initiate.

Ukraine was obliged by its allies to observe the ceasefire. Russia, on the other hand, did not feel obliged to conform, and this attitude and their ongoing attempts to break the ceasefire terms was to lead to a serious situation on the battlefield. The Russian President had regarded Ukrainians as Russians who had forgotten who they were and had assumed that a gentle reminder, backed by a display of military might, would remind them of their heritage and draw them back to mother Russia. He had expected his troops to be accepted, even if not with open arms. He was therefore surprised by the hostile reaction of the population and especially by the outright rejection of his motives by the Ukrainian Government and military. He was also alarmed at the rapid support given to Ukraine; economic, political and military; and defeats of his army in Kyiv, Kharkiv and Kherson. His initial goal of political subjugation with a benign Russian military presence left in situ had to be dramatically amended. The invading nature of his 'Special Military Operation' was creating problems. The Russian population, seeing economic decline, loss of personal well-being and persistent and spreading rumours of battlefield setbacks, despite overwhelming propaganda constantly proclaiming victory, became more restive. The spread of knowledge of returning body bags caused him to modify his targets. These now became the total subjugation of the Donbas, which would allow him to declare victory. To allow this, a minimal military aim was to take over the whole of the Donbas region. At the time of the ceasefire there remained a large salient occupied by the Ukrainian Army between Severodonetsk and Donetsk. Despite the ceasefire, the President of Russia needed to see this salient removed. He had to break the ceasefire agreement to achieve this. NATO and the other powers supervising the ceasefire had to react.

Within ten days of the start of the ceasefire, Russian forces therefore began aggressive military attacks on Donetsk, and also missile strikes at Kyiv and Lviv. Russian artillery was positioned within the Donetsk area borders and missiles were launched from Russian territory, from the air and from Russian Black Sea ships. If the ceasefire was to be meaningful, the response from the supervising powers had to be equally meaningful. NATO felt obliged to react.

Breakdown of ceasefire and coalition response

By our Correspondent in Kyiv

The ceasefire agreement between Russia and Ukraine was being broken. Russian belligerence called for military responses by the coalition. Russia's actions indicated that it still posed a threat and was a reminder of the possibility of a renewal of its original war aims. This threatening behaviour provided the catalyst required to ensure that the coalition would continue to pull together rather than lose its enthusiasm and cohesion, which was a danger as allied nations grappled with their own domestic problems. NATO reinforced its garrisons in the Baltic states so that each had the equivalent of a reinforced armour division. The UK commanded in Estonia, France in Latvia and Germany in Lithuania. The US presence in Poland was increased to a minimum of two marine divisions and the coalition joint air force was increased to a minimum of four hundred aircraft with support services and relocated at a number of Polish air force bases. US Patriot air defence missile systems were positioned to cover the Ukraine borders, backed up by a range of other air defence missile and radar defensive systems. NATO was, in effect, reminding the Russian President that his original strategic aim to keep NATO forces away from Russia's western border had achieved the reverse effect. NATO was now very much stronger on its east border than had ever been envisioned. Meanwhile, Ukraine had taken its opportunity to re-arm its military, especially its army, and had reinforced its frontline positions along the line of Russian encroachment in the Donbas and Southern Ukraine Black Sea areas.

The coalition, very early on following the ceasefire agreement, had, through the United Nations Secretary General, arranged an approving vote in the General Assembly to action, by force if necessary, aimed at clearing the Ukrainian port of Odesa to allow grain carriers to use the port. Turkey had been the principal agent in allowing mine clearance in the seaways to Odesa and arranging for the release of the twenty-five million tons of grain held by Ukraine in Odesa and desperately needed by hungry nations, especially in North Africa and Asia.

All of this was background to the continuing bellicose statements being issued by Russia. A demonstration of Russia's aim was the build-up of Russian forces in the Donbas area, reinforced by the call-up of reservists creating a position at least as threatening as the situation presented prior to the invasion of the 24th of February 2022. A resumption of all-out warfare appeared to be imminent. The coalition had to be prepared for this. A coalition meeting attended by all participants, and especially EU/NATO, was arranged.

Observance of ceasefire conditions

A further statement by the coalition supervising the ceasefire – a press release

The coalition takes note of the further loss of civilian and military lives caused by renewed aggression by the Russian Federation. It regards such loss as unconscionable. If it goes unanswered, it will be repeated, including the absurd claim that the Ukrainian military are to blame. NATO has therefore responded militarily.

The ceasefire terms promised retaliation in the event of aggressive actions by the Russian Federation. The coalition believes that such retaliation is necessary and will be repeated if further aggression takes place. The source of the offensive fire has been determined as within the Donbas area but also from Russian naval vessels in the Black Sea and from within Federation territory, by missile and from aircraft. The coalition recognises that in taking countermeasures against these targets and by attacking Russian territory, the level of conflict is being internationalised and has become a direct conflict between NATO and other coalition countries, and Russia. This is regarded as a dangerous intensification of levels of hostility, but Russia seems to accept this in order to achieve its strategic goals. NATO will respond as required and is immediately strengthening its military capability in the Baltic countries and Poland, including the Suwalki Corridor, in anticipation of some form of threatening behaviour, especially against Estonia, bordering Russia. The coalition has expressed its views in a letter copied below:

To the President of the Russian Federation

Dear Mr President,
It is internationally recognised that you initiated the war with Ukraine and continue to provide it with momentum. Despite the ceasefire, a number of aggressive actions have been carried out by forces under your command: Lviv, Kyiv, Kherson and Donetsk have been attacked from the air, sea and land.
These attacks break the terms of the ceasefire and, under those terms, we, the supervisory coalition, must respond. Such a response could lead to direct military attacks on assets you control. Such action is regrettable but necessary to preserve the ceasefire. Such action will not be taken if you provide assurance, within twenty-four hours, that all acts of aggression from forces which you control will cease. Otherwise, regrettably, we will be forced to act.

The statement continues ...

> The following message has been received from the Russian Federation:
> The President has received and denies the accusation that the Federation has carried out the actions you describe. We assert that all the incidents you list were carried out by the Ukrainian military in order to ferment conflict. We will continue to observe the principles of the ceasefire.

Coalition military support of ceasefire

By our Correspondent in Kyiv

All retaliatory activity was carried out by air strikes and was kept to a minimum. Three artillery units in the Donbas area were destroyed, as was a single mobile missile launcher just inside the Russian border. One airfield runway within Russia was bomb cratered and one strike aircraft destroyed on the ground. A missile launcher on a ship close to Odesa was damaged. No attack countermeasures directed at our aircraft were detected. These limited targets were attacked to demonstrate force capability, and as a warning that further infringement of the ceasefire would be met with enhanced response as appropriate.

Should China arm Russia?

A paper by China Forward

We are concerned about the potential consequences of the close bond of friendship declared between China and Russia when their presidents met just prior to Russia's invasion of Ukraine. No treaty was published but both presidents declared their intention of providing close and long-term support to each other.

Russia saw their declaration as providing major political support in justification of its forthcoming assault on the established rules for the maintenance of international law and order. China saw their partnership as a geopolitical gain to support its continuing confrontation with the USA, especially its position in relation to Taiwan. Initially, it saw the intervention of NATO and the USA as a benefit in diverting political, military and financial attention away from its own imperial activities. China's attitude to Russia's war in Ukraine is genuinely uncomfortable. It abstains from UN motions calling for Russian withdrawal and provides Russia with financial backing and non-offensive material. It also benefits from being able to buy oil and gas from Russia at discounted prices, which would normally have been sold to western Europe. China has, however, become alarmed at the very poor performance of Russia's army in Ukraine. It now has to react to Russia's ongoing request for the supply of offensive military equipment.

Russia's army in Ukraine is using up stocks of equipment dating from the Soviet era. Its quality and condition is very poor in comparison with the NATO equipment now being provided to Ukraine. The Russian General Staff must have been aware of the sub-standard means at its disposal, but the short campaign envisaged by the Russian President would have been accommodated. The prolonged resistance of the Ukrainian Army, using relatively sophisticated NATO material, has caused a major problem for the Russian Army. It finds it increasingly difficult to mount effective offensive operations. It is very much in need of assistance from China.

China Forward's concern is to consider and comment on the options available to China and their consequences. From the start of the war, NATO, and especially the USA, have been very positive in urging China to refrain from providing Russia with any offensive equipment. The penalties arising consequent on so doing have been stated as being extreme in financial and economic terms. Additionally, the opprobrium reflected in UN motion votes condemning Russia must be taken into account. What should China do? We pose this question bearing in mind our concern over the maintenance of China's northern and western borders, currently cushioned from any possible aggression by geographical Russia.

Limited Support The supposition here is that, given no more than adequate discreet and limited support, Russia will be able to maintain an occupying position in Ukraine which will allow it to declare a victory. This will require the maintenance of a significant military garrison and the subjugation of a population and an aggrieved Ukrainian government still wishing to recover its stolen land. There will be no move on a ceasefire. Russia will remain threatened by a NATO still supporting Ukraine and a Russian state suffering a progressive social and economic decline. This will eventually lead to an internal revolution and a possible rapprochement with the West. This is a highly undesirable outcome for China given that it will already have been severely criticised internationally and would now suffer painful penalties from the West and supporting countries. This policy is not recommended.

Unlimited Support China is capable of supplying all the material which Russia would need if it were to launch a new and effective assault on Ukraine. It would take time for a major re-equipping of the Russian Army to take place. NATO would be forearmed and would extend and reinforce its support to Ukraine accordingly. Given the very significant extension of the conflict, it is very possible that NATO tri-service forces would be directly involved. In effect, a major war would have commenced, with China an obvious adversary. China would also find itself involved in a possible coincident conflict in its Asian sphere of interest. Such a possibility must surely be out of the question. This course of action could not be recommended.

Conclusion It is therefore considered by China Forward that China can have little say in the outcome of the war in Ukraine. It must await the outcome and prepare itself to mount its own defensive military operation in eastern Siberia as proposed in a previous paper. Russia has done China no favours by mounting its 'Special Military Operation' in Ukraine, except for creating an obvious opportunity for China to regain its lost territory in eastern Siberia and mould the geopolitical position in Siberia more to its advantage.

CHAPTER SIX

Resumption of Hostilities

**Russia tries and fails to make progress in the Donbas
and towards Moldova. China Forward expresses
concern at the vulnerability of China's effective western
border protected by Russia.**

Russia in Ukraine: Resumption of Hostilities

The Current Situation on Ukraine's Eastern Border

Russia in Ukraine: Resumption of Hostilities

By our Correspondent in Kyiv

Russia and Ukraine have taken time off hostilities to refurbish, reorganise and re-equip themselves. In the meantime, Russia declared to its people that it had succeeded in its 'Special Military Operation'. In fact, it was a long way short of its limited declared military and political objectives (having failed to take Kyiv). A very significant element of those objectives was to control the whole of the south Black Sea coast of Ukraine, including the coastline as far as Moldova, originally part of Imperial Russia and therefore included in its ambitious aim of recreating the empire's territory.

Moldova has a small population, about three million people. A partisan uprising had freed it from Soviet rule in 1989. However, the newly freed country was left with a sliver of territory along its eastern border, retained by pro-Russian separatists and supported by Soviet troops who remained there after the creation of free Moldova. The strip of territory is called Transnistria, garrisoned by about one thousand five hundred Russian soldiers.

Russia now had Moldova in its sights. To reach Moldova it had to reclaim Kherson, taken and lost in a later phase of Russia's war, and also Odesa, lying between Kherson and the Moldovan border. Both cities had been heavily fortified in expectation of such an advance. The move west proved to be problematic for Russia. The approaches to Kherson allowed tank and accompanying armoured personnel carriers easy going, but they were now met by GPS guided missiles, fired by new launchers provided by the USA and UK. These allowed missiles to be guided accurately onto Russian armoured columns, inflicting heavy casualties. Newly provided 155mm artillery pieces also inflicted great damage. Well-prepared ambush positions, manned by infantry armed with anti-tank hand-held launchers, also played their well-rehearsed role of piecemeal destruction of tanks and personnel carriers, especially when urban built-up areas or areas of close country were encountered.

In order to achieve what had been hoped to be rapid progress, the Russian advance had not been preceded by the usual tactic of reducing urban targets to rubble using artillery, prior to an attack. On the contrary, attacking forces were now confronted by sophisticated artillery and missile launchers capable of inflicting significant damage. The balance of firepower had moved in favour of the Ukrainian defenders. This improvement also applied to attack from the Mig fighters, bought from countries around the world and fitted with low- level attack guided missiles from the NATO armoury. Russian ground attack aircraft continued to rely primarily on unguided iron bombs. Russia again failed to gain air superiority in Ukrainian air space and continued to provide inadequate air support to its ground forces.

Fighting around Kherson continued for about a week, but the Russian attacking force was unable to make meaningful headway. Losses suffered in their attack made them susceptible to counterattack after their initial attack was repulsed. They were driven back some kilometres east of their start point. Russian forces now also attempted to renew their offensive in the Donbas by striking north towards Izyum, with the intention of joining up with a force attempting to retake Kharkiv. Despite the major effort put into rebuilding their army, they found that the force levels they were able to deploy were still inadequate to cope with a rejuvenated Ukrainian army now equipped with adequate quantities of large-calibre artillery and long-range guidance ground attack missiles. Enhanced attack from the air and continuing drone attack added to their problems. The force levels available to the Russian attack were no longer capable of gaining ground against determined Ukrainian resistance. The moves against Izyum and Kharkiv advanced no further than their start lines.

The third planned Russian offensive was another attempt to close the Donbas salient between Luhansk and Donetsk by attacking from south and north. Here, the Russian columns met with positive defeat. The Ukrainian

Army had anticipated this action and had assembled a considerable combined arms force with the intention of recovering lost territory. In this case, a Ukrainian armoured column, supported by artillery, moved eastwards against light opposition with the aim of reaching the Russian border to the east of Luhansk. After four or five days of fighting, this was achieved. Russian forces in the Donbas area were split in two and a portion of the eastern Ukrainian border was recovered.

As a consequence of these various actions, Russian forces had been fought to a standstill, losing territory and becoming divided. The Russian Army had been effectively defeated and was in no position to conduct any further aggressive action. As far as the remainder of Ukrainian territory was concerned, a major improvement was achieved as a consequence of the receipt and deployment of 'Iron Dome' anti-missile equipment from Israel and anti-air missile launchers from Germany. They were very effective in reducing the number of missile strikes launched by Russia against civilian and infrastructure targets, to the point that they were thought unrewarding and stopped.

Ukraine was at relative peace. It had been accepted as a candidate for membership of the EU and NATO. A second ceasefire had been negotiated and Russia was considered to be in a frame of mind to accept its withdrawal from occupied Ukraine, including Crimea, so long as the sanctions imposed by the West in 2022, and now causing unacceptable damage to Russia's economy, were removed. This arrangement had to be negotiated between Russia, Ukraine, the EU and NATO. This would take time but could be achieved.

The current situation on Ukraine's Eastern border

A paper by China Forward: Beijing

For whatever reason, be it a truce, ceasefire, or simply a pause in operations, the level of violence in Ukraine, and especially in the Donbas area, has been considerably reduced. Recent missile strikes by Ukraine have been very successful in destroying Russian ammunition stock piles, reducing the effects of artillery bombardment and causing slow-down of Russian operations. Ukraine is very grateful for a temporary halt to Russia's slow advance. Russia is showing every sign of running out of the means and willpower to continue the offensive, at least in the short term. It appears to have used up a very large part of the resources, including ammunition and missiles originally allocated to its 'Special Military Operation'. To assemble, equip and launch a renewed attack may be beyond its capability in the short term. It is faced with unrest in the areas it has captured, doubts about the reliability of Belarus, Dagestan, Ingushetia and Chechnya, and the new threat, posed by the creation of a new and hostile border including Finland and Sweden. This border now runs from the Baltic to the Black Sea.

China Forward is very uneasy about the ability of Russia to sustain its western border should the EU and NATO, for whatever reason, become aggressive. It can no longer be assumed that Russia, in the depleted state in which it now finds itself, could defend that border. It is a long way from China but is in fact China's western border. In the past, we have assumed that Russia would always be able to protect that border. We now wish to emphasise the point that this assumption can no longer be taken for granted. We have also, in previous position papers, postulated the possibility that the border could lie within the area of EU/NATO responsibility should Russia decide to join those organisations. This may seem an unlikely event but we have to remember that Russia is a European nation and that the possibility has to be considered. We are concerned about the long-term strategic implications of such an event and we alert the government of China to our concerns.

CHAPTER SEVEN

China Revisits the Treaty of Aigun

The 'Unfair Treaty of Aigun' is mentioned in the People's Congress and diplomatic exchanges between China and Russia raise China's interest in reclaiming its land.

Time to Reverse Aigun

Meeting of China's People's Congress

Communications between Russian and Chinese Governments

China Principles Applicable in Negotiating Position in East Siberia

Briefing by China Forward: Time to reverse Aigun

A press briefing recorded by our Correspondent in Beijing

I remind journalists in the audience that China Forward is a totally independent think tank which funds itself through contributions, including the fee we have charged you for attending this briefing. We are free of any government interference and can express our views without fear of consequences. We achieve a consensus within our own system and publish the truth as we see it and any obvious lessons and desirable actions which emerge. Given our location and background, we speak principally of situations likely to affect China and, hopefully, gain the ear of government authorities in so doing.

This briefing is the outcome of our rising concern over the unfolding situation surrounding Russia and the foolish adventure it embarked upon in Ukraine. In the spring of 2022, the Chinese President and the Russian President made a very public display of new and deep affection between Russia and China. Internationally, China is acknowledged as being by far the stronger of the two economies whilst also being in an increasingly economic, political, social and low-level military confrontation with the USA. Russia is seen as a decaying economic lightweight but with a strong centralised autocratic government with a very large military establishment, ruling over a vast country (Siberia) and, importantly, in possession of a very large nuclear arsenal. Siberia provides a stable northern border for China and counterweight to the strength of the USA. This interdependent affection provides a strategic depth to the aims of both countries, with promises of mutual assistance.

Russia's adventure in Ukraine has revealed how one-sided this partnership is. Russia's dependence on hydrocarbons for its livelihood has highlighted its current and long-term weakness and susceptibility to the effects of western-led sanctions. Also, its very poor military performance in being driven to stalemate by a country one third of its size very much reduces its value as a strategic partner.

Russia has brought upon itself a situation quite the reverse of what it intended. Instead of creating a buffer between itself and NATO, it now has a virtual front line which stretches from the Baltic to the Black Sea. NATO's doctrine believably states that it has no intention of entering Russia itself, but the latter now has a very long border along which it has to plan for a possible confrontation. This will consume a large part of its military strength on a permanent basis. The strain already imposed on Russia is evidenced by its need to reinforce its army in Ukraine by weakening its strength in Kaliningrad, Transdniestria, the Caucasus and East Siberia. Its alleged ability to protect the whole of its Siberian territory can now be regarded as untrue. This reveals east and north-eastern Siberia as potential areas of strategic weakness, given the location of a strong USA combined arms capability in north-eastern Siberia. If confronted with the weakness of its strategic position, Russia would presumably claim that its large population, residual military capability and hydrocarbon and mineral wealth will allow it to recover from its current position of weakness. However, the enmity it has generated across the world, its continuing assertion that it intends to recover its lost empire, the continuation of sanctions and its very poor current economic performance mitigates against that ambition. Sanctions imposed on Russia may be lessened in time and its overseas markets restored, but its path to a healthy economy will be long and difficult. Its very much lowered profile will be its feature for some time to come. Any imperial ambitions it has must now be abandoned if it is to live in peace with its neighbours and restore its international prestige.

The strategic problem facing China has to be addressed. The solution has long been in hand and should now be implemented. This takes us back to the Treaty of Aigun. Before 1858, China had, very loosely, controlled land to Lake Baikal in the east, in the Amur valley and habitable land north of that area. China and Russia at that time had minor and intermittent contact in a rather vague area between the Amur valley and the Arctic Ocean. This huge area provided China with the buffer space to protect it in the north. Russia stole that area in 1858/9. It is now necessary to recover it.

We have previously pointed out the necessity, in China's strategic interest, of reversing the territorial loss resulting from Aigun. We have previously stressed that, given Russia's then apparent strength and especially its nuclear armoury, a delay would be wise. We were concerned that Russia could effectively brandish its nuclear arsenal to deter China. The events occurring in Ukraine have demonstrated that the Russian President frequently issues threats of a nuclear response to actions taken by NATO and as frequently has stepped away from action. We have previously discussed the high-level political discussion which would be required to call the Russian President's bluff, should he threaten a nuclear option. This discussion would include consideration of the likely response of the USA should the President of Russia consider the nuclear option. We consider that the USA would thwart any such option by including its own nuclear capability in the balance of options. NATO has now absorbed these threats and, by the promise of overwhelming retaliation, we believe, has nullified the Russian President's threat. The time has therefore come to rectify the consequences of Aigun. We expect Russia to attempt to negotiate a solution but we believe that none, short of total renunciation of the Aigun Treaty, should satisfy China. We believe that, given the current very weakened state of Russia, the return of the lost territory to China would be accomplished relatively easily. Should Russia attempt to resist any consequent military incursion by China, our expectation would be that Russian defences would be quickly overcome.

We recommend that China take action now.

Comment by our correspondent

It is inevitable that China will wish to negotiate with Russia the return of its lost northern territories. If the current President is still President then it is also inevitable that he will decline to offer anything meaningful to China. Such action would contradict his aim of expanding Russia, not reducing it. Some level of confrontation is therefore likely. This confrontation would have a significant effect on Russia's position in its own continuing quasi-war with NATO. As a consequence of Finland (and Sweden) joining NATO, and given Belarus's ambiguous alignment, Russia has a front line with NATO which it has pledged to protect. The bulk of Russia's field army will thus be concentrated in the west, leading to further depletion of its force in Siberia and, in particular, eastern Siberia. It has always been very questionable that Russia's garrisons in the east would provide any meaningful resistance to a Chinese invasion. The concentration of Russia's capability in the west makes successful containment of a Chinese invasion even less likely. Chinese annexation of East Siberia could be quickly accomplished. Russia would have a major problem in stopping a Chinese advance without seriously weakening what it would have come to regard as a defensive position against NATO in the west. At that point, it is quite likely that the Russian President, and his failed policies, would be removed from power. NATO and the West generally would have to decide how to control the now diminished Russia and confront China's success in the east.

Attitude of the USA

Very much linked to the position postulated above is the likely attitude of the USA to any move by China. This is discussed in a separate paper.

Comments by our defence editor

China Forward does produce some original ideas but it cannot be assumed that everything it publishes will have been approved by Central Government. However, it must be assumed that the principle of recovery of China's lost northern provinces is being raised somewhere within government and must therefore be of concern to Russia currently occupying those provinces.

China's People's Congress

By our Correspondent in Beijing

The People's Congress, meeting every spring, brings together the upper echelons of government and communist party functionaries from the whole of China. It is attended by around three thousand people. Its purpose is to hear and – always – approve the plans of central government. The principal speakers take questions which are approved in advance and are always related to government policy. One of the questions asked at this year's Congress reads as follows:

> China has now emerged from many years of poor economic and military health to be a nation powerful enough to contest any other nation on earth. We have regained our position as a leading power in the world and especially in Asia. In years past, our weakness led to the imposition of treaties which benefitted other nations but were unfair to China. Many of these treaties have been corrected, for example, the recovery of Hong Kong and Macau, and unfair terms of trade granted to mainly European countries have been cancelled. However, one significant unfair treaty remains in force. That is the Treaty of Aigun, reinforced by the Convention of Peking of 1860, which removed a large section of the Chinese Pacific coastline and over one million square kilometres of Chinese territory; annexed to Imperial Russia. My question is: Will China now negotiate with Russia to arrange the return of annexed land?

Minister's Reply

The existence of the unfair Aigun Treaty is recognised. It has long been the ambition of China to renegotiate the treaty. Given the historic weakness of China until recent years, and the fact that Russia has, on the whole, been a good neighbour, the Chinese Government has refrained from raising this issue with the Russian Government. Russia remains a good friend, and the Chinese Government has no plans to raise this issue at this time. However, the Government recognises that the pride and economy of the Chinese nation were hurt by the terms of the Treaties of Aigun and Peking and will raise the matter with the Russian Government at the appropriate time. I thank the delegate for raising this issue, which will be close to the hearts of all delegates assembled here who, I am sure, will support the Government's response when appropriate.

Communication from the Russian Government to the Chinese Government concerning matters raised at The People's Congress

A statement issued by the Russian Foreign Office

The Russian Government values its close political and economic ties with the Chinese Government and wishes that these continue into the future. Its view of the Aigun Treaty is that it represented the wishes of both countries at the date of signature, and both benefitted from it. In particular, it allowed the Chinese Government to concentrate its economic and military capacities, quell dissent within its territory and reduce any further erosion of its control of the China Sea coastline. Russia benefitted from its access to the Pacific and built up significant infrastructure and population concentrations in the territory.

The Russian Government believes that these declared benefits served, and continue to serve, both countries well and does not therefore recognise any need to change the arrangements agreed at Aigun. It will, of course, be willing to discuss any minor adjustments that will improve the current warm relations between the two countries and looks forward to any agreed discussions with pleasure.

The Aigun Controversy: Diplomatic Exchanges
A Beijing note issued by the Chinese Government

Art. 1 From the Chinese Government to the Russian Government
We share the desire for peaceful relations between China and Russia but wish Russia to understand that the annulment of the Aigun Treaty has long been a national goal. The treaty was signed under the threat of force at a time of Chinese weakness. These times are past. China is strong and wishes to reclaim its inheritance.

Art. 2 From the Russian Government to the Chinese Government
China wishes to overturn Russia's rights to what is, legally, its land. This request is rejected. Russia will defend its territory and the Russian people who live there. We ask China to desist from making these unreasonable claims.

Art. 3 From the Chinese Government to the Russian Government
We regret Russia's attitude towards what we now regard as occupied Chinese territory. We ask for negotiations to arrange a new treaty in which we would agree to the rights of Russian settlers, on what is Chinese land, to be respected but we can no longer accept sovereignty by Russia over our land.

Art. 4 From the Russian Government to the Chinese Government
We much regret the hostile tone of the current Chinese response. A new treaty would be unacceptable. We see no need for renegotiations on the sovereignty of what has been Russian land since 1858.

Art 5 From the Chinese Government to the Russian Government
China wishes to maintain good relations with Russia and will seek to negotiate despite Russia's initial rejection of our offer. We will present our negotiating position in due course. It is also necessary to say that China will follow due procedures where colonial issues are concerned and we will present our case to the United Nations if appropriate.

Proposed principles to be included in any negotiations with Russia concerning China in East Siberia

A press release by China Forward – Report by our Correspondent in Beijing

This paper suggests an outline of the principles which would find favour with the Chinese people who are very hostile to the continued occupation of Chinese lands by Russia.
　　The negotiations should cover:

1. The land covered by the Treaties of Aigun and Peking
2. The area north of China reaching to the Arctic Ocean

Treaties of Aigun and Peking The land ceded to Russia in 1858 stretched northward from the Chinese border to the west of the Stanovoy Mountain chain. The area included territory to the north of the River Amur and north-east to the Gulf of Tartary as far as the northernmost point of Sakhalin Island. South of the Amur, the land ceded lay to the east of the

River Ussuri, east to the Sea of Japan and in the south to Vladivostok and the border with Korea. This land area was to have been jointly administered by China and Russia. This caveat was largely ignored and was, in any case, superseded by the Convention of Peking which ceded the whole territory to Russia. The total land mass annexed to Russia exceeded one million square kilometres. At this time, the Island of Sakhalin was divided, with Russia gaining the northern half and Japan occupying the south. Russia annexed the whole island in 1945. It is the view of China Forward that the whole of the territory described above should be returned to China. The future of the largely Siberian (Russian) population of the area would need to be subject to negotiation. It is anticipated that all those wishing to remain under Chinese sovereignty would be welcome to stay. The transfer of material assets belonging to the Russian state should be agreed in a negotiated settlement. All Russian military, air and naval forces would be required to leave. A significant increase in population as a consequence of Chinese population movements should be expected. Chinese military garrisons would necessarily reoccupy all facilities vacated by Russia. The return of the occupied lands would provide China with a cushion of territory to its north. In particular, the Stanovoy Mountain range provides a good defensive frontier. The possession of the ice-free ports on the Sea of Japan, and the possession of the coastline itself, provides protection from any seaborne incursions from the Pacific Ocean. In the south of the area, the acquisition of full control over the Amur River, which is navigable from its estuary, allows its use by military craft. The possession of the Trans-Siberian Railway and its road network provides protection from incursions from the west. Thus, in repossessing over a million square kilometres of territory, China gains a large measure of protection to its north.

In our view, the area which we have described must now be extended. The treaty area does not provide for a defensible border to the west. Medieval China controlled an area to the west at least as far as Lake Baikal, until it was forcibly occupied by Tatar adventurers. The lake provides a natural and defensible border and should therefore again become the Chinese border in the west. This proposal should be included in negotiations with Russia.

The Area to the North of the Stanovoy Mountain Range
This area is becoming of increasing interest to China because of the effects of global warming, which is creating navigable shipping routes skirting the northern coastline of Siberia and passing through the Bering Straits, which

separates Russia from the USA state of Alaska. The freeing up of sea access to the northern Siberian coastline creates, in effect, a new sea border. China must take a long-term view of the potential threat this creates and plan accordingly. Objections are anticipated from the USA (Alaska) and from the Buryat people living south-east of Baikal and the Yakuts of Sakha. China Forward has stated its view that Russia is a declining empire. Its recent adventure has highlighted its already limited capability and capacity to defend itself. In particular, its control over its vast Siberian hinterland has been made much more unsure. We believe that the totality of Russian land mass has become indefensible. If Russia fails to defend its borders, then China's borders are also at risk. China must now consider the land between Lake Baikal and the Arctic to be of strategic concern. These conclusions must surely be in the minds of Russia's strategic planners. However, we repeat our belief that Russia is, and will remain, incapable of defending this vast area and thus, in effect, protecting China's northern border. We believe that these northern areas should now be annexed to China. We do anticipate that the USA will strongly object to the takeover of a large area adjacent to its Alaskan border. We anticipate that the area will have to be shared with the USA, which will also require existing ethnic settlements to be taken into account.

CHAPTER EIGHT

Siberia and its People

The people of Siberia resent Moscow's control of its resources and potential wealth. Independence would be welcome.

Siberia: An Appendage to Russia

An Independent Siberia

Siberia: An appendage to Russia

By our Foreign Affairs Editor

Siberia covers thirteen million square kilometres. A traveller moves through eleven time zones to get from Moscow to the Pacific. This area is inhabited by about twenty-eight million people. There are four administrative and geographically identifiable zones. The Urals mark a district boundary between European Russia and the mass of Siberia, with a population of twelve million. This steppe land is marshy and includes much of Russia's industrial capacity and also much of its gas and oil resources. The middle area is the Siberia Federal District, largely steppe with Mongolia on its southern border and a population of twenty million, mostly living along its southern border. The East Federal District, with a population of seven million, borders China to the south and the Pacific Ocean to the east. Its tip is the Bering Straits, with Alaska on the far side. Most of the original ethnic Siberian population lives here. It numbers about five million, split between at least forty ethnic groups speaking different but related languages. Of these, the widest spoken language is Mongolic with about four hundred thousand speakers, Yakut with about four hundred thousand and Tuvan with two hundred and forty-five thousand. The concentration of these ethnic groups was brought about by Stalin in the 1930s, wishing to remove potentially hostile peoples from more salubrious territory along the River Amur, preferred by Russian settlers, and to break up and fragment possible organised objection to his rule. Stalin was equally hard on two or three million Germans, Poles, Ukrainians, Baltic peoples, Crimean Tatars and other nationalities within Russian peripheral territories where potential dissent could be troublesome. To be added to the total are at least one and a half million political and routine lawbreakers who spent much of their lives in Gulag prisons.

The fourth district of note is the area around Lake Baikal which had, at one time, been the western boundary of Chinese Imperial authority before the advent of Russian imperialism. Thus, the population of Siberia numbers about thirty million; 85% are of Russian extraction with the balance of four and a half million of different ethnicities. In discussing the social and political attitudes of these populations, it is of note that Russian and other races settled in central and east Siberia tend to regard themselves as, and are called, Sibiriaks, who are distinctly less loyal to Moscow than it would like. Siberiaks have an independent attitude towards Moscow, which is regarded as a bullying and aggressive taskmaster, stripping Siberia of its wealth and providing very little in return. For instance, 70% of exported oil and 90% of exported gas comes from Siberia, in total providing about 60% of total Russian exports. Siberiaks resent this. Mass protests have occurred but Moscow (and the President) suppressed them quickly and media criticism is banned. Siberia is no stranger to oppression by Moscow but this was not always so. Siberia was ruled by Turkic and Mongol peoples from the start of the first millennia and remained so until Genghis Khan conquered the whole of Siberia in the thirteenth century. The khanate set up by Genghis, called Sirbir, lasted until the late sixteenth century, by which time Muscovy had expanded to be a more powerful Russian state, in about 1508 moving against Sirbir and destroying it as a state. Very rapidly, Russian adventurers moved across the Urals fur-trapping and harassing the much weaker ethnic tribes they met; these were ill-coordinated, poorly armed and could not resist the Cossack intruders. The latter were vicious and genocidal in their treatment of the clans they came across, adopting a policy of mass killing, stealing all possessions and killing the reindeer herds which were life-sustaining for these nomadic peoples. Many clans were obliterated and the remainder driven north to less hospitable climes. Stalin completed the process started by the Cossacks during his purges in the 1930s. Cossack adventurers, supported by the Russian state, reached the Pacific in the mid 1850s, at the time of the Aigun Treaty. The Trans-Siberian Railway was completed between 1891 and 1905 and Russia was now in control of the whole of Siberia. Russian governments have always been sensitive to the vastness of Siberia and their control over it. The very rapid growth of China and its sheer size highlights their reason for being sensitive.

An independent Siberia

By our Foreign Affairs Editor

Siberia has a land area of 13 million square kilometres, with a population of 3 persons per square kilometre: the lowest population density of any nation on earth.

A mix of Turks and Mongols inhabited the area from the first millennia; hunter- gatherers living off fish and reindeer. Genghis Khan interrupted this lifestyle by occupying much of Siberia and installing a khanate which survived for about 200 years, paying tribute to the Russian state which eventually took over their lands as part of Russia's expansionary movement east through Siberia. By the early 18th century, Russia occupied, thinly, the whole of Siberia up to the lands governed by China in East Siberia.

Early settlers were always troubled by the need to pay homage to Moscow. The first call for independence was made by Mikhail Bakunin in March 1863. The first attempt at achieving this condition arose as a consequence of the turmoil surrounding the Russian Revolution in 1917. A White Russian government, supported by troops from the Chinese Empire Qing dynasty, was established in Tomsk. This government, called the Provisional Peoples' Assembly, appointed ministers, controlled a significant part of eastern Siberia and raised an army of 10,000 troops which initially defeated a Red Army sent to oppose them. By 1920, the Red Army had gained the upper hand and the Peoples' Assembly was dispersed. Through the 1930s and in particular as a consequence of Stalin's reign, Siberia was used as a dispersal land in which to relocate the original inhabitants comprising about 45 ethnic groups, largely from southern Siberia to eastern Siberia. They were dispersed and broken up into minor groups with the clear purpose of limiting dissent. From the 1930s onwards, they were joined by captured soldiers and political dissenters housed in Gulags as punishment. They were used as builders of local infrastructure. At least two million persons were detained in this way, including hundreds of thousands of Ukrainians, Poles, Germans and Baltic peoples. These swelled the ranks of Russians imported to populate the southern area of Siberia, mainly to stimulate agriculture. By the 21st century, the population of Siberia would number about twenty

million, over four million of ethnic origin, with the balance made up by
Russian settlers and by inter-marriage between Russian settlers and other
people of European stock. Of the DNA to be found amongst the Siberian
population, 80% is of European extraction and 20% Asian. Russian settlers
always regarded themselves as free of serf ancestry and somewhat superior
to western Russians. They called themselves Sibiriaks. This feeling of
superiority has persevered and is represented in a constant demand for at
least autonomy if not independence from Moscow. This search for a greater
say in their affairs is highlighted by the knowledge of how much West Russia
depends on their endeavours: 80% of the revenue from Siberian exports is
retained by Moscow. This revenue is obtained from the output of gas, oil,
metals, minerals, silver, gold, diamonds, wood and pulp products. Only a
minor proportion of this revenue is fed back into Siberia, to meet social
costs and the building of infrastructure. Further ire is caused by the
knowledge that 80% of all tax raised in Siberia is retained in Moscow.
Siberia's people feel neglected by Moscow and are made to feel like colonial
subjects. These feelings are reflected in the constant call for more freedom,
including fair and transparent elections. This spirit of independence was
reflected in rallies held in 2014 to protest at the annexation of Crimea, a
reflection of the fact that a significant portion of the original Tatar
population of Crimea had been banished to Siberia by Stalin.

In 2013, an exhibition extolling the virtues of a United States of Siberia was
held in the University of Novosibirsk. Frequent rallies and demonstrations
were held elsewhere in Siberia to seek a United States of Siberia. Siberian
federal governors were elected until 2014, but from then on they were
appointed by Moscow. As a consequence, the Siberian population now finds it
very difficult to make its voice heard. All rallies and demonstrations are
banned. The Russian President has stated his concern that they could be used
as a pretext for foreign interference in Siberia and therefore in Russian affairs.
He appears to have a genuine concern about the stability of this vast area on
which Russia depends for much of its economic health, but shows little
concern for the well-being of its people. The people of Siberia, be they ethnic
or Sibiriaks, have a low regard for western Russia and believe that they would
gain much benefit if freedom from Moscow control could be achieved.

Note
The geographic boundaries of Siberia as discussed above will be addressed
separately.

CHAPTER NINE

China in the United Nations

China is criticised by many nations for its imperial
ambitions and actions but receives support for its
confrontation with Russia. The United Nations Assembly
also criticises, by implication, China and Russia for
absorbing the territory of other nations and claiming
their populations as their own.

*A UN General Assembly Meeting to Discuss China's Claims
in East Siberia*

*Collective Comment by Nations Peripheral to the South
China Sea*

South China Sea: India Comments

The UN Commissioner Comments on Xinjiang

*UN General Assembly: Discussion of Requisition of Rights in
South China Sea*

General Comment on China's Position

Security of Nationality

UN Vote on Nationality Security

A UN General Assembly meeting to discuss China's claims in East Siberia

By our New York Correspondent

The Chinese Government filed a motion for debate at the General Assembly which reads as follows:

The territory occupied by the Chinese nation has remained
largely unchanged for thousands of years. A major exception to

this continuity is the large area north of the River Amur in the north-east of China, north of the province of Heilongjiang. In 1858, this province was annexed by Imperial Russia in a treaty forced upon China as a consequence of military threat. During the same period, the territories of Hong Kong and Macau were ceded to European powers. The latter two territories have now been returned to China peacefully, after negotiation. The land north of Heilongjiang remains in Russian control and Russia has refused to negotiate its return to China. The Chinese Government now wishes to apply pressure to force Russia to abandon its unfairly and illegally gained land and seeks the approval of the General Assembly to allow China to take any reasonable action necessary to regain its land.

The Russian representative to the General Assembly presented the case for Russia's retention of the province, based on the legality of the Treaty of Aigun and the subsequent Russification of the territory. The envoys of Member States, and other peoples under Russian control who would prefer to be free of it, were also invited to speak. A summary of what was said is shown as follows:

Comment made by Ukraine
The President of Ukraine addressed the General Assembly

My country of forty million people is, as you are aware, a member of the United Nations. So is Russia, but that country decided to invade my country on the 24th of February 2022, without cause. Its president declared that his aim was to free my country from a fascist government (mine) and also that my country did not deserve to exist and should be absorbed into Russia. My people object to this. So far, about forty thousand civilians have paid for their objection with their lives, as have many of my soldiers. Russian guns and rockets have pounded many of my cities to rubble, destroying homes and associated infrastructure. It will cost hundreds of billions of dollars to rebuild, but the lives of the dead have gone forever. The Russian President's actions have also led to the death of even more of his own soldiers and damaged the well-being and livelihoods of his own citizens. In addition, he has used the threat of withdrawing basic food supplies of grain to the humanity of the world, as a means of putting further pressure on my country to accede to his demands. I am sure that his own people would deny him the moral or political right to do what he continues to do in Ukraine, but his propaganda system denies them the right to even know what he is doing. The Russian President is an evil monster. He should not be allowed to continue to lead his people into war. He thinks nothing of invading another country by claiming, without any legal or moral basis, what he believes to belong to Russia. On the same basis, China should now be allowed to reclaim what is rightfully theirs. It also goes without saying that the invaded lands of Crimea, the Donbas and the Black Sea coast of Ukraine must be returned to the Ukrainian nation, as soon as possible.

Comment made by Kazakhstan

A Statement by the Kazakhstan Ambassador to the United Nations

I speak for the President of Kazakhstan who wishes to complain about the very high-handed treatment of my country by Russia, our much bigger neighbour. Our relations are generally workable but Russia has a tendency to ignore our interests, in pursuit of its own. For instance, we are perfectly entitled to sell our oil to western Europe and we are in the process of doing this despite pressure from Russia not to do so. Likewise, we have found that our grain requirements, normally supplied by Russia, have for some reason been delayed. I am not going to express an opinion on the merits of China's claims in East Siberia, but I take this opportunity to invite Russia to take more care of its relationship with neighbouring countries if it seeks their support.

Comment made by the envoy from Dagestan

My country includes fourteen ethnic groups, mainly Muslim but also including Jews and Christians. As a representation of the Avar, the main ethnic group in the country, I speak to the Assembly on behalf of all ethnic groups. Multi-ethnic Dagestan is a harmonious multi-cultural state. Each group has its own language plus some Russian and respects it and other groups' cultural heritage. A referendum was held in 1993 which led to calls for a parliamentary system of government, but that was rejected by the Central Government in Moscow and has not progressed further. The people of Dagestan have a strong memory of the war fought between themselves and the Bolshevik Red Army in 1920/21, which led to the incorporation of Dagestan as a federal state within Russia. The people of

Dagestan would welcome the freedom to run their state for their own benefit and inevitable betterment. We wish to achieve this condition at some future date and, meanwhile, support China's legitimate claim for repossession of their own land.

Comment made by the United States of America

The USA has always upheld the right of people to free themselves from tutelage and choose their own form of government. The USA agrees the generally held view that the lands now being claimed by China were seized by Russia under threat of the use of military force. The USA agrees that the Treaty of Aigun must be regarded as unfair treatment of China and should be revoked. We trust that this will be achieved as a consequence of negotiation, leading to arrangements that would avoid the possibility of conflict.

Comment made by Great Britain

As a country which, in the form of the British Empire, controlled a quarter of the world's population from London, we have reason to be proud of the benefits which we have given to the world, but we are also proud of the manner in which we shed our responsibilities. Despite the mistakes we made, we gave freedom to many of the nations which now sit amongst you. We are firmly of the belief that Russia should now free itself of the consequences of the unfair Treaty of Aigun and allow China to reassert its proper authority.

Comment made by Chechnya

I am Islam Belokiev and I represent an armed unit leading a nationalist movement which seeks the independence of Chechnya from the Russian Federal State. We fought the Russian Army in 1994 and again in 1999. At first, we were successful and formed an autonomous republic, but an overwhelming Russian attack forced us from the battlefield in 1999. Our capital city, Grozny, was very badly damaged by the Russian Army, and a dictator nominated by the Russian President, the President of Chetnya, was forced on us. We have recently re-formed our military wing and are again attacking the Russian occupying army. Our aim is independence from Russia, and anything which weakens that country and ultimately allows us our freedom is very welcome. We support China in its effort to reverse an illegal occupation. We would welcome any support which would help us to remove the Russian occupier from our country.

Comment made by Georgia

I speak as a representative of the Georgian Government. We declared independence from Russia in 1991 but have been in almost constant conflict ever since. The conflict is based on the fact that the Georgian provinces of Abkhazia and South Ossetia, which include small Russian populations, have resisted attempts by the central Georgian Government to integrate them into our population. Russia has recognised both territories as independent republics, which now claim to be part of Russia's federal state. The level of support offered to dissidents in both territories by Russia led to an invasion of Georgia by Russian military units, which penetrated some distance into Georgia before withdrawing. Thus, two significant areas of Georgia, from which two hundred to three hundred thousand Georgian people were evicted, remain under Russian control, with quasi-referendums held to confirm their absorption into Russia. Russia used brute force to exercise its power beyond its borders. Russia historically exercised this same power in acquiring land in East Siberia. Now that there is a possibility of a reversal of its occupation of that land, it should be implemented. Georgia supports the motion.

Comment made on behalf of Estonia, Latvia and Lithuania

I speak as the permanent representative of Estonia on behalf of all three countries collectively known as the Baltic states. We were freed from German occupation in 1944 by the Russian Army. We were grateful for that but as a form of tribute Russia then arranged for significant numbers of Russian nationals to arrive in our countries as immigrants. The integration of the incomers into our native populations has not been without its problems, but we, and they, constantly attempt to improve on the level of integration achieved. This is not helped by Russia's continuous attempts to interfere with our well-being. The most obvious method is to hack our IT systems, controlling everything from bus networks to power stations. This interference seems to be based on the principle that any Russians living outside Russia's national borders have to be controlled and, according to principles which Russia lays down, to be protected. This 'protection' includes the threat of incursion by their military if they think it convenient. Fortunately, we are members of the EU and NATO and gain confidence from that position. However, the degree of bullying involved seems consistent with the level of bullying which led to the forced signing of the Treaty of Aigun in 1858/9. We therefore support China's effort to reverse the outcome of that treaty.

A statement made by a representative of groups ethnic to Siberia

I am a Buraty by ethnic origin. My people number about four hundred and fifty thousand, which represents about 10% of the forty-five groups making up the ethnic population of Siberia. The next largest ethnic group by size are the Yukuts, who number about two hundred and fifty thousand. My people make up a third of the Federation Republic of Buryatia. There is about the same proportion of Yukuts in the town of Irkutsk. The original inhabitants of Sibir consist of forty-five groups or tribes. They speak a variety of languages based mainly on Turkic dialects.

I speak for the four and a half million ethnic origin people living in Sibir. Most tribes originally lived in the south of Sibir and in the plains to the north. All my people were deported by Stalin in the 1930s and forcibly settled in scattered pockets of population, dispersed so as not to create potential unrest aimed at the Russian Soviet regime. In the process of forced migration, many people had to surrender their property. They were not allowed to take their reindeer herds, which were stolen from them. We were forced to rebuild our lives wherever we found ourselves and owe nothing to the Russians who deported us. Time has allowed a healing process and we have intermingled with the Russian settlers, the Sibiriaks, who are now almost ethnic settlers themselves. We, and they, would welcome any break from the overpowering Russian state which misuses us. We welcome the prospect of removal from Russian vassalage and support China in its attempts to free its own land.

A statement made by the Japanese Government

A treaty ended the Russian/Japanese war in 1905. Both countries had claimed the island of Sakhalin as part of their territory prior to 1905. The treaty confirmed that Russia would control the northern half of the island; Japan, the south. In 1945, at the end of the Second World War, Russia invaded Sakhalin, overpowered the small Japanese army there and annexed the whole island, together with the Kuril Islands; historically, Japanese land. Russia has retained ownership of both Sakhalin and the Kuril Islands since that time by occupation rather than right. On a number of occasions, Japan has invited Russia to discuss ownership. Russia has declined to take part in talks. This refusal confirms Russia's frequent historically noted habit of seizing land by military force and then absorbing it into Russia rather than returning it to its rightful ownership. We desire the return of Sakhalin and the Kuril Islands and support any action which might lead to that conclusion. The UN motion is supported.

Objections raised against China in its dispute with Russia

By our Correspondent

A representative of the littoral nations of the South China Sea and a spokesperson representing the Uyghurs of China asked that their treatment at the hands of the Chinese state be raised by pointing out that China, in seeking to correct historical injustices metered out to weaker nations, should be called to account for the injustices it currently forces on its neighbours and even on its own people (the Uyghurs) in Xinjiang and the South China Sea. It seems to want its cake and eat it. In my view, feeling was widespread amongst Assembly members that any concessions granted to China should be balanced with concessions in areas where it is using its superpower ability to seize what it wants. There was a feeling that voting patterns would reflect the criticism being expressed increasingly forcibly. Furthermore, that the nations granting China its wishes should express the concern of the international community over China's behaviour and also to specify conditions to be met by China if the motion is passed.

Collective comment by nations peripheral to the South China Sea

From our UN Correspondent

I am the Indonesian Ambassador to the United Nations. I speak for the nations on the periphery of the South China Sea who have reason to complain about the overbearing attitude of China towards these nations. China claims that a notional line called the 'nine-dash line' represented the outer limits of what it claims to be its territorial waters. It claims all fishing and mineral extraction rights within that line. A UN-appointed tribunal declared this to be unlawful in 2016. China has rejected this finding. The majority of international opinion agrees the finding. The littoral nations naturally accepted the judgement, especially as the nine-dash line frequently crosses their own two hundred-mile limit. In order to enforce its alleged rights, China has commenced requisitioning uninhabited rocks and sand bars inside other nations' territorial limits and constructing military facilities, including harbours, airfields and permanent buildings. Some offensive weapons have also been introduced. China has, in effect, extended its military power base in a way that threatens the security of the littoral nations. This is unlawful and unacceptable. The nations I am representing today will never accept this infringement of their territorial integrity. Our nations will shortly present a motion to the General Assembly which will require China to desist from its actions.

This statement has been formulated during discussions related to China's requests for support in seeking the overturning of the principles of the Treaty of Aigun. I now formally state that the nations I represent will vote against this motion and any other motions stemming from it, unless China formally renounces its claims in the South China Sea, based on its nine-dash line. I have circulated a paper providing more details of the situation I have described.

South China Sea

A statement made by the Indian Ambassador to the UN

China claims most of the South China Sea within what it calls the nine-dash line. This includes all sea areas less coastal waters of peripheral countries, including Brunei, Taiwan, Indonesia, Malaysia, Vietnam and the Philippine Paracel Islands, the Scarborough Shoals and areas in the Gulf of Tonkin and Natunta Island. Its claim includes rights to fishing, oil and gas but also, more importantly, strategic control over the sea. To reinforce its claim, it has enlarged and fortified islands in the Spratly and Paracel groups. Areas of dispute with other nations include the Vietnamese coast, an area north of Brunei, the South Sea Islands mentioned, north of Natuna, west of Palvana and Luzon, Sabah and the Luzon Strait. In July 2016, a UN-appointed tribunal ruled against China in a dispute with the Philippines. China's claim was based on an original claim made by Japan in 1930 and later claims made by pre-Communist China and by Communist China in 1947 and 1958. The UK, Germany, France and the USA have rejected China's claims, and the great majority of international opinion agrees. Clashes have occurred with India, Vietnam and the Philippines. The USA regularly conducts naval patrols through the sea to reinforce international claims for access to what is widely regarded as international waters. Also, in particular, the USA, Indonesia, Vietnam, France, Japan and the UK intend to reinforce the claims for open access by repeated naval patrolling.

India is part of the Asia Pacific Quadrilateral Security Dialogue (the QUAD agreement), which aims to ensure free and open maritime access on the basis of a rule-based maritime order. The other countries are the USA, Japan and Australia, which conduct joint exercises in the designated area. The UK and France join these exercises as appropriate. The aim of the QUAD is to limit the expansionary nature of China's naval and military activities in the area and preserve its international characteristics. China's predatory inclinations must be restrained. India will support China in its aim of recovering its lost lands but India will also support the Indonesia motion calling on China to restrain its imperial expansionist activities. India is concerned that unrestrained aggression by China could ultimately lead to conflict with countries around the South China Seas and also with the broader international communities concerned with retaining the international nature of the Seas.

A statement from an official from the office of the UN Commissioner for Human Rights, speaking for the population of Xinjiang

From our UN Correspondent

Xinjiang is an autonomous province of China, with a population of about twenty-five million. The ethnic Muslim Uyghurs make up about 50% of the total population, a proportion being reduced by Han Chinese immigration. Most Uyghurs are concentrated in the East Turkestan region of the country. The balance of the population is mainly of Han Chinese origin, located in Southern Turkestan. The Chinese Government encourages migration of ethnic Han peoples to Xinjiang to dilute the proportion of Uyghurs.

The country has plentiful resources of minerals, including oil, gas and coal. Only about 10% of the total national area is habitable. The Qing dynasty ruled the country until taken over by the PRC: People's Republic of China. At the turn of the 20th century, unrest spread across East Turkestan. This was fed by separatists wanting greater freedom from the control of the central Chinese Government and was encouraged by the spread of a form of radical Islam. A few Han citizens were killed and police stations attacked.

The central government decided to introduce a form of strict control over the movement and day-to-day routines of ethnic Uyghurs. Police raids were frequent and many were arrested without good cause. Many Uyghurs were deported to mainland China and forced to work in factories. They were effectively kidnapped. These oppressive activities reduced the level of violence within the community, but the most significant measure of control introduced was the creation of what can only be described as prisons, where over a million, mostly male Uyghurs, continue to be incarcerated. The Chinese authorities claim that these are educational centres, teaching basic literacy skills. The disciplinary methods employed are brutal, with beatings, mild torture and isolation cells commonly used. These institutions cannot be visited by outsiders, and especially journalists.

Nevertheless, information on what is happening in these prisons leaks out and a UN driven investigation was started, led by the UN Commissioner for Human Rights. The UN report was finally published on 1st September 2022. This detailed the inhuman treatment carried out by guards at the prisons. This, combined with the very harsh routine treatment of Uyghurs in general, in the view of the report amounted almost to genocide. China immediately denounced the findings of the report and linked it in part to the USA specifically and to the West in general attempting to belittle China. The report is a major stain on the reputation of China, harming it throughout the world. The Uyghurs have no vote on the motion before you, but I ask that you bear in mind the plight of the Uyghurs before you allow the Chinese state to trample on them and on any other ethnic groups, including those in East Siberia.

China's unlawful requisition of rights to areas of the South China Sea

A motion proposed for discussion by The General Assembly

Sponsored by Indonesia and supported by the Office of the Secretary General

In 2016, a tribunal sponsored by the UN ruled that China's pronouncement, that the area of the South China Sea contained within its self-declared nine-dash line was China's territorial sea by right, was unlawful. China did not accept the ruling. The rest of the world objected to the conversion of an international sea into Chinese territory. Furthermore, other nations, in particular the USA but in fact all nations with an interest in the navigable use of the sea, stated their intention to ignore the Chinese edict. Regrettably, China has since decided to attempt to impose its control of the area claimed by constructing military installations on uninhabitable rocks and shoals within the area, thus creating islands based on sand accumulations where none existed before. Their installations intrude in many cases into the territorial waters of littoral nations.

This motion requests that China respects the findings of the UN tribunal, accepts that its requisition of international waters to be its own is unlawful and removes all military installations erected in international waters.

The motion was put to the vote.

General comment on China's position

By our UN Correspondent

In talking to leaders of less prosperous countries, I have found a surprising level of suspicion regarding the overbearing attitude China takes towards them and a level of caution expressed in contemplating financial agreements with China. The Belt and Road Initiative (BRI) launched by China has been successful in drawing countries into China's orbit. Roads, bridges and harbours have been built at Chinese expense and loans given to countries in need of capital. The infrastructure provided has been beneficial, but the loans have frequently been at quite high levels of interest and infrastructure projects are often used by China as collateral against the loans. Chinese funds have been easy to obtain, but repayment has become a problem for many countries. The easy money provided has frequently become something of a debt trap. China is increasingly asked for debt write-off or improved terms. China tends to drive hard bargains in those circumstances. Those national leaders already embroiled in the debt payment problem are providing real-time lessons for other capital-seeking nations. Western-backed organisations such as the International Monetary Fund (IMF) or the World Bank are regarded with renewed interest by impoverished countries. I write this to record my view that China is becoming increasingly regarded as authoritarian and bullying and a country to be approached for favours with caution.

One upshot of this situation is that China's motion seeking support for its quest to have the Treaty of Aigun reversed is that fewer countries are likely to support it than expected. The depositions from countries that have suffered at its hands, especially South China Sea littoral nations and the people of Xinjiang, will count against it. Also relevant is the debating motion now put forward by Indonesia, inviting China to respect the findings of the UN tribunal. This called China's claim to territorial ownership of most of the South China Sea unlawful, and required removal of all military facilities built there. The motion will win with a significant number of nations supporting it. The same outcome is expected on the motion sponsored by China on the Aigun Treaty. China will win support but by a small margin, which will trouble it when it moves into a confrontational situation with Russia.

UN Assembly vote on the unlawful Chinese Claim of Rights in the South China Sea

For the Motion	:	102
Against the Motion	:	59
Abstained	:	20

The motion put forward by the Indonesian delegation was won. In essence, China is being invited to conform with the findings of the International Tribunal and desist from claiming territorial waters in the South China Sea.

Voting on The General Assembly Discussion on East Siberia – The Reversal of The Principles of The Treaty of Aigun, Sponsored by China

For the Motion	: 109
Against the Motion	: 20
Abstained	: 52

The motion put forward by the Chinese delegation was passed: Russia's position gained very little support. Approval is given to China's attempt to reverse the principles of the Treaty of Aigun but the high abstention rate was noteworthy.

Security of Nationality: A Statement

A note from the office of the Secretary General of the United Nations

It has been noted that world peace is being compromised by a growing tendency for major nations to take advantage of lesser powers to invade land on their boundaries and, subsequently, claim it as part of their territory. The justification for these claims is provided post facto by arranging a referendum amongst the population, aiming to show that the majority supports the annexation. Such referendums are too easily arranged to give feasible outcomes and should not be used or trusted. My office will now introduce a motion to be debated by the General Assembly, which will aim to suppress this undemocratic activity.

Note by our foreign editor

This is not a new problem. It has been given prominence by the very blatant recent and planned use of referendums concerning nationality created by Russia. The most obvious was a vote arranged and carried, allegedly by a majority, for the incorporation of Crimea into Russia. Russia has promised the same for areas occupied in Ukraine; in particular, the Donbas, Luhansk and southern Ukraine, including Kherson. Similar moves are planned for South Ossetia and Abkhazia in Georgia. The settings for these referendums are areas within countries that border Russia, which has encouraged and frequently forcibly enforced settlement by ethnic Russians. The areas in which settlement takes place are those which Russia has been able to detach from the mother countries by military intervention; for example, Ukraine, or by arranging and supporting minority local nationalists to take up arms against their own governments, for example, South Ossetia. The areas concerned then claim sovereignty and expect Russian political and military support if required. Outstanding examples of potential problems are the three Baltic states: Estonia, Latvia and Lithuania. All three have significant ethnic Russian minorities forced on them by Russia, which overran these countries after driving out the German Army in 1945. All three countries are now members of NATO and are thus protected from overt intrusion, but covert interference in national affairs continues, for instance, by hacking into systems controlling internal infrastructure such as telephone networks and power grids. Other areas liable to suffer potential intrusion are countries in the Caucasus, Kazakhstan and Mongolia. In all countries, Russia claims the right to interfere if, in its view, the rights of Russians are being abused. Thus, Russia is surrounded by countries and statelets in which it claims an inherent right to intrude if it thinks it expedient to do so in its own interest. This creates a situation of almost permanent antagonism vis-à-vis European countries which might consider providing assistance to these beleaguered entities if requested. This is all an extension of the desire of the Russian President to rebuild the glories of the historic Russian Empire as he sees it.

The UN General Assembly has now been asked to vote on this issue.

Security of Nationality: A motion put before the General Assembly of The United Nations

This Assembly wishes to ensure that security of nationality is preserved, in that any segment of any nation is properly consulted when a change of nationality is being proposed, for whatever reason, by a neighbouring state. It is proposed that a change of nationality can only be accepted by a majority of the population. It is further proposed that the preparation of voter lists, the conduct of the referendum and the proclamation of the result will be organised by a body arranged by the Secretary General's office. The result will be reported to, voted on and carried by a simple majority of the UN General Assembly.

The motion was passed.

For the Motion	:	156
Against the Motion	:	12
Abstained	:	13

A footnote by our Foreign Affairs Editor

The vote reflects international resentment at the way in which Russia plans to extend its borders; that is, by invasion followed by annexation. Ingushetia, South Ossetia, Crimea, Kaliningrad, Transdniestria, Donbas, Luhansk and Kherson are prominent examples. The principles outlined in the motion express moral and political outrage. The proposal is unlikely to achieve just ends; certainly, Russia will ignore them. But they represent a world in which most people wish to live, and represent pious hopes rather than practical realisable views, at least in the short term.

CHAPTER TEN

China invades Siberia

Following the UN Motion related to Aigun, China
invades Russia (Siberia). Following the Battle of Amur,
the Russian Eastern Army retreats towards Lake Baikal.

Russia/China Negotiations

Russian/Chinese Foreign Ministers Meet

China: Special Military Operation in Siberia

China's Incursion into Siberia

NATO Intelligence Briefing on the Battle of the River Amur

Battle Maps

Action subsequent to UN General Assembly Sessions and Russia/China negotiations

From our Beijing Correspondent

Subsequent to the meeting of the UN General Assembly, the Chinese Government invited the Russian Government to initiate talks to discuss their mutual positions. The Russian Government responded by saying that its position was clear and that it was inconceivable that Russia would surrender its eastern Siberian territories. Since the UN meeting, China had been building up its military strength on its border with Russia, along the Ussuri and Amur rivers. On being questioned by our reporter in briefing sessions held by the Chinese Foreign Office, it was stated that China had no intention of entering Russian territory and that the forces' build-up was part of a long-planned training exercise. It stated that the same comments applied to the significant build-up of Chinese naval forces in the Gulf of Tartary and the Sea of Japan.

Comments by our defence correspondent

The statement made by the Chinese Foreign Office is a repeat of the frequent statements to the same effect issued by the Russian Government prior to its invasion of Ukraine. It is almost a comic parody of that situation and, if anything, indicates an intention to proceed in the same way. Russia is being warned.

The Foreign Ministers of China and Russia meet

Press releases by China and Russia covering negotiations

Press release by China

Russian (later General) Murayev arrived at Argun in 1858 at the head of fifteen thousand soldiers. China's provincial governor possessed no military force beyond his personal household and guards. Murayev demanded he sign a treaty of cessation, which he was forced to do. The treaty granted Russia over six hundred thousand square kilometres of Chinese land, north of the River Amur. The annexation was confirmed, by China, at the Convention of Peking 1860. At that time, British and French troops had occupied Peking and were establishing bases along the South China Sea. China was forced to cede Hong Kong and Macau to Britain and Portugal respectively, in addition to granting custom-free concessions at Chinese coastal cities to European powers, Japan and the USA. An additional four hundred thousand square kilometres of land was ceded to Russia, south of the River Amur and east of the Ussuri River, including Vladivostok. China has always, and still does, regard the transfer of land by military coercion as unfair, both legally and morally. China wishes for the annulment of the treaties and the return of the land to China. China recognises that Russia, and a significant number of its people, have established economic and social roots in the lands described and offers concessions to smooth the transfer process. China would expect all Russian state holdings of property, infrastructure and financial assets to be transferred to China, but it is content to allow civil populations and their personal property to remain and be absorbed into the Chinese state. China will compensate for the value of personal property acquired by China to allow good government and also to allow the living space required by large numbers of Chinese citizens who expect to emigrate to the newly acquired lands. All Russian military and police garrisons and equipment from all three services will be expected to be removed within one year of the signing of an agreement. The area of land covered by this agreement is described and mapped on the annex to this agreement.

Russia is reminded that one hundred and thirty million Chinese live within the provinces adjacent to the current border. The Russian population to the north of that border numbers about eight million. China points out that the demographics of East Siberia will inevitably lead to a very large migration of ethnic Chinese to East Siberia within a short time frame. Russia is invited to note this demographic inevitability and accede to China's request for the repudiation of the Treaty of Aigun to allow the peaceful demographic changes to take place.

Press release by Russia

Russia is not persuaded that the Treaties of Aigun and Peking are illegal. They were approved by both parties, who signed in the full knowledge of their scope and outcomes. Moral issues do not enter into this discussion. Russia has legally occupied the lands discussed since 1858/60. This legal basis allowed for the development of infrastructure and urban entities to house a significant population. Russia is not prepared to surrender what it has created and will resist any attempt, peaceful or otherwise, to achieve this change. The President of the Russian Federation has personally briefed his government that any attempt to change the situation to the detriment of Russia will be resisted by whatever means are required. He also states that no further negotiations are to be conducted. Only abandonment of China's claims will resolve this issue.

China: Special Military Operation in Siberia

From our Correspondent in Beijing

It is no real surprise that today China launched a major military invasion into Russian Siberia. It moved across the border south of Khabarovsk with three major thrust lines. The total force numbered at least four hundred thousand personnel, including over one thousand five hundred tanks and two thousand other armoured vehicles. Major air battles immediately erupted. The Russian Air Force was significantly outnumbered and outclassed, with China expected to obtain air superiority within days. One armoured thrust bypassed Khabarovsk to the east and headed north for Komsomolsk to the east of the River Amur, heading for the Baikal Amur main railway line and intended to clear Russian forces from the Pacific coastline along the Gulf of Tartary. The second column aimed to invade Khabarovsk and cut the territory in half by heading for the Pacific at Samarga. The third thrust was to the south, cutting off any Russian forces operating north of Vladivostok and invading that city. The Chinese forces were in overwhelming strength in relation to the East Russian Army, and all three thrusts achieved their objectives in less than twelve days. The East Russian Army had been depleted to reinforce the invasion of Ukraine, and what remained was retired to the west of Khabarovsk to fight another day.

Initial Chinese incursion into Russian Eastern Siberia

By our Defence Editor

A Chinese army of about four hundred thousand personnel, including at least one thousand five hundred tanks, two thousand other armoured vehicles and five hundred artillery pieces with supporting arms, had been assembling in Manchuria around and to the east of Harbin for at least eight weeks. The build-up had been well documented by spy satellites. The Russian East Siberia Army had been concentrated south of Khabarovsk, partly protected by the River Ussuri on its right flank and the sea on its far left. Vladivostok at the southern tip of the Primorsky oblast, surrounded on three sides by the sea and on the Chinese border, was very difficult to defend, but national pride demanded that an attempt be made. Thus, it became invested by Chinese forces, with about ten Russian battle groups with armour remaining in the city and its environs. The Russian Army was not sufficiently prepared to repel the Chinese incursion. All its equipment, including tanks, was outdated and no match for the relatively new equipment of the Chinese Army. The Far East Army had been a backwater for many years, and its equipment, quality of manpower training and leadership, reserves of equipment, repair and medical facilities, communication equipment at headquarters and unit level and especially general logistic backup, were sorely lacking. The situation had been considerably worsened by the need to strip the army of much of its effective combat ability, of infantry, armour, artillery and logistic support to replace losses and reinforce the battered army in Ukraine. What remained was an army of conscripts with poor-quality equipment. The Far East Air Force was generally equipped with old MC29 and Foxglove fighter aircraft which allowed the Chinese Air Force to quickly gain air superiority. Russian equipment was mostly semi-obsolete, with very little guided weaponry. Russian forces deployed in the oblast were subjected to heavy unchallenged air attack and lost many of their tanks and light armour to such attacks. It was an army in name only. The Russian President has assumed it to be secure within Russia's borders with no obvious military challenges. An attack from China was not expected, although a constant nightmare scenario for his more prescient generals. The Eastern Army was no match for the modern, well-equipped and numerous Chinese forces to its south. Russian forces retreated to the Khabarovsk area. The River Amur, very wide at this point, provided a stop line to defend. The city itself was largely east of the river and was defended in the same way as Vladivostok, with about ten battle groups remaining in the city, with a further fifteen battle groups initially deployed on the River Amur and then retreating to the west. The Russian high command was reconciled, as was the German Army in Stalingrad in 1944, to creating siege conditions for these portions of its army marooned in Vladivostok and Khabarovsk: about twenty thousand soldiers in all, in the expectation of returning at a future date and relieving the siege. This proved to be wishful thinking.

Overall Chinese strategy

The ongoing semi-confrontational situation between China and the USA in the South China Sea will have been a major influence affecting China's decision to invade Siberia. A possible invasion of Taiwan was a preoccupation of the USA and its allies. A significant element of China's military was now committed to its role in East Siberia. Whilst being only relatively lightly tested by weak Russian resistance, it had to protect itself from any possibility of counterattack whilst also garrisoning its new territory. It could thus be assumed that any invasion of Taiwan had at least been postponed. This situation would provide relief to Taiwan and also to NATO, including the USA, with major commitments assigned to defending Western Siberia.

The Reaction of The USA to the Chinese Invasion

The USA was not prepared to allow the region of north-east Siberia, across the Bering Straits from Alaska, to fall into hostile or even neutral hands. The USA, therefore, immediately on hearing of the Chinese invasion of Siberia, despatched military units to secure what it would regard as a significant territorial barrier between Alaska and any possible Chinese encroachment. The USA, therefore, claimed jurisdiction along the 160° line of latitude from the Arctic Ocean and including the whole of the Kamchatka Peninsular. In particular, it occupied all Russian military installations in Kamchatka, including ports and airfields and Russian military installations in the north-east area facing Alaska. It positioned minor units along the 160° latitude. It anticipated that all territory south of the 160° line would become part of a new nation accommodating existing ethnic minorities.

Intelligence briefing given to war correspondents at NATO HQ, Belgium

By our NATO Correspondent

Order of Battle

At the time of China's initial incursion into eastern Siberia, Chinese forces available to engage with Russia are shown below. Also shown is the equivalent order of battle available to Russia in East Siberia, which had already been considerably reduced by the reinforcements sent to Ukraine.

	Combat Personnel	Tanks	APCS	Helicopter	Aircraft	Artillery
China:	1.10 million	3,500	2,500	900	1,500	7,000
Russia: (Eastern Army)	250 thousand	1.000	1,500	250	500	2,000

China's incursion rapidly overwhelmed Russian forces around Vladivostok. At the end of the first week of operations, it controlled all Russian territory south and east of the Amur River. In response to the incursion, Russia ordered the evacuation of all military units from Sakhalin Island and concentrated the army around Khabarovsk, north up the Amur River as far as Komsomolsk and along the river as far as Belogorsk. It did not abandon Vladivostok but left a garrison (tanks and infantry) of ten battle groups in and around the city (about ten thousand personnel).

A Comment on The Battle of The River Amur

By our Defence Editor

Neither the Russian nor Chinese Governments are prepared to allow other nations' journalists to enter the war zone. We are thus dependent on either government providing detailed information, based upon its own view, on the course of the war. We do, however, have contact with army and civilian individuals within the Russian defence establishment, who provided this newspaper with general but newsworthy information before hostilities commenced and continue to do so now, albeit in an abbreviated form as the war progressed. We were also able to establish communications with civilians in the combat area who were frequently able to provide us with voice and image information. We drew on the very large pool of satellite imagery provided by the USA via their satellite network. We were therefore generally well informed on battlefield progress: in war, grey areas are numerous and inevitable, but a clear story emerges from the almost inevitable progress made by the Chinese. NATO has particularly good satellite imagery, which tells its own story and is passed to defence correspondents regularly.

Intelligence Briefing: Statement issued by NATO Headquarters. The Battle of The Amur

A press release

The Chinese moved rapidly, having enveloped Vladivostok and pushed north against light opposition across the width of Russian-held territory. At the same time, they launched a major offensive from south of the Amur, with the main thrusts aimed at Birobidzhan, Blagoveshchensk and Belogorsk, all places on the Siberian Railway. Garrisons in all three towns were recently reinforced in anticipation of a Chinese attack, and troops who traditionally guarded the frontier along the River Amur, using watchtowers and behind barbed wire, were also available. However, the Chinese were able to choose their point of crossing the Amur and thus to concentrate their forces. There were bridges across the Amur at Leninskoye, Amurzet and Obluche, and there was main road and bridge access up to the border at Blagoveshchensk. In any case, the Amur, whilst wide and shallow, was relatively easy to cross, with pontoon bridges at many places, and this occurred.

The air forces of China and Russia were initially evenly matched in numbers, but superior Chinese aircraft quickly gave the advantage to China, and Russia was unable to maintain any form of air superiority. It was able to fly enough reconnaissance sorties to confirm the Chinese crossing points over the Amur and move forces to defend them. Russian forces concentrated around Khabarovsk were quickly deployed along the Amur to do this. The main Chinese thrust was up the G1211 road heading for Blagoveshchensk, supported by two pontoon river crossings to its east. The road network to the east of Belogorsk was widespread and provided ease of movement once the river was crossed. Over two hundred thousand soldiers supported by five hundred tanks and twelve hundred other armoured vehicles were deployed, split between three attacking columns.

Russian forces moving west from Khabarovsk had to travel six hundred kilometres in total to reach the battle area, but they had the advantage of the railway and a good road to travel on, and were reinforced by the combat army based to the west of Khabarovsk. It took the Chinese force over three weeks to assemble their attacking columns. Thus, the Russian forces had adequate time to prepare, although without air superiority they suffered significant casualties as they deployed. The main battle became a tank battle around Blagoveshchensk which went on for four days. In the end, the Chinese prevailed as a consequence of tight control of their formations compared with the problems facing the Russians, in particular because of poorly organised logistics, bad communication between units, too-frequent mechanical equipment breakdown including tanks, and poor morale amongst the conscripted soldiers. The outcome for the East Army was a somewhat disorganised retreat to the west, leaving behind about ten battle groups tasked with the continuing defence of Khabarovsk.

The retreat of Russian forces to the west benefitted from their defence of the west bank of the River Selenga, which flowed north to south through Blagoveshchensk. Bridges over the river were destroyed forcing the Chinese to mount river-crossing operations under direct fire. This caused a delay to their westward advance of ten days. Moving west of Belogorsk, the retreating army gained protection from the River Zeya to the north and the River Amur to the south. The only east-west route available to the Chinese was the combination of the Siberian Railway and the G121 running alongside it, and both could be blocked by defensive positions prepared by the Russians at will. However, they were outflanked by the Chinese able to move along the G202, a road running inside their own territory. The westward move of the Russian East Army was therefore reasonably orderly but relatively hurried. The intention of the army was to establish a defensive position at Amazar and Ignashino.

10

Nagorsk &
Talnakh

River Lena

Se

Kachug

Ust-
Ordynskiy

Irkutsk

9

This battle map commences
on page 89

Ulan-
Ude

7

M O N G O L I A

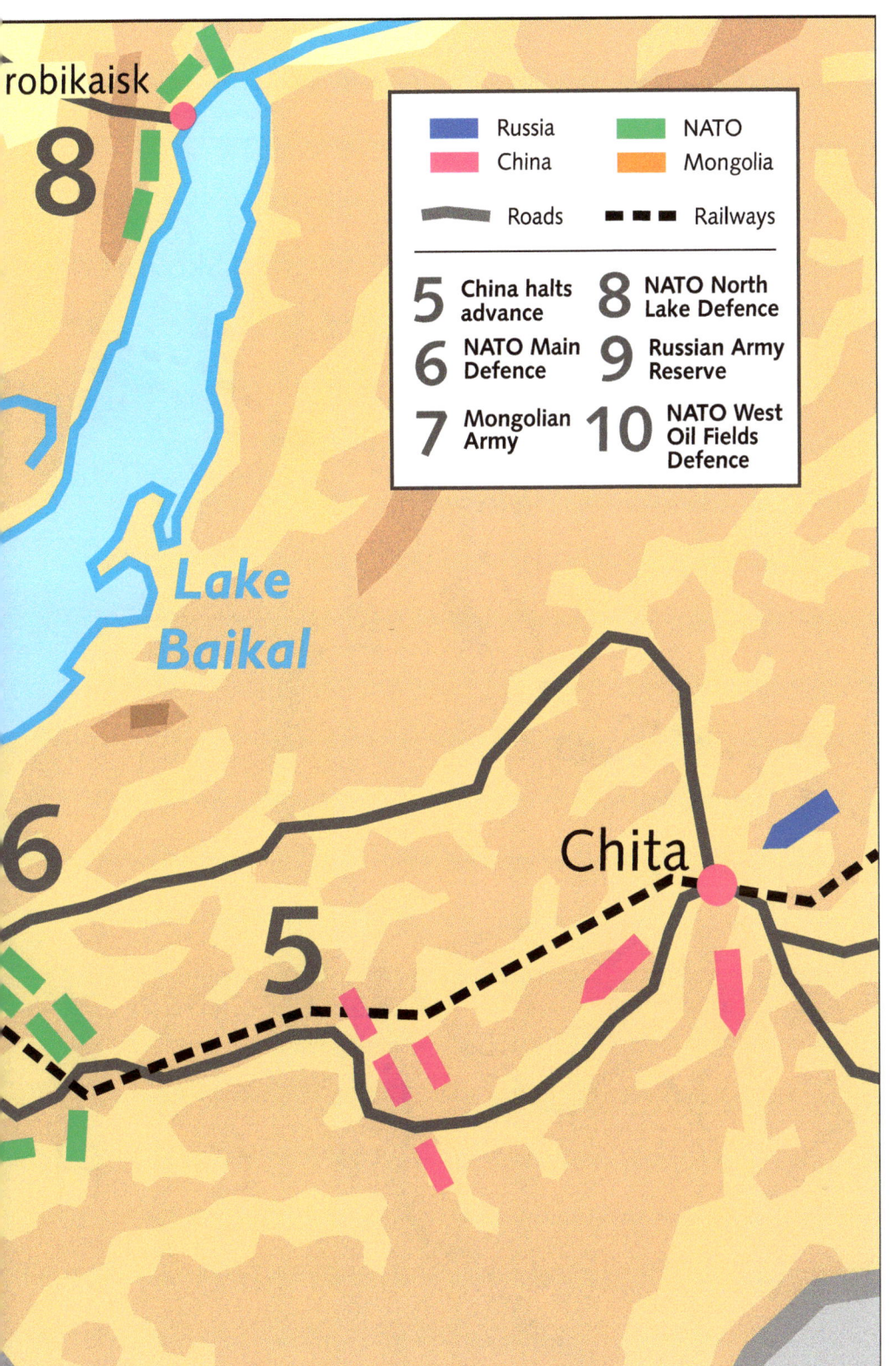

robikaisk

8

Lake
Baikal

6

5

Chita

Legend:

- Russia
- China
- NATO
- Mongolia
- Roads
- Railways

5 China halts advance
6 NATO Main Defence
7 Mongolian Army
8 NATO North Lake Defence
9 Russian Army Reserve
10 NATO West Oil Fields Defence

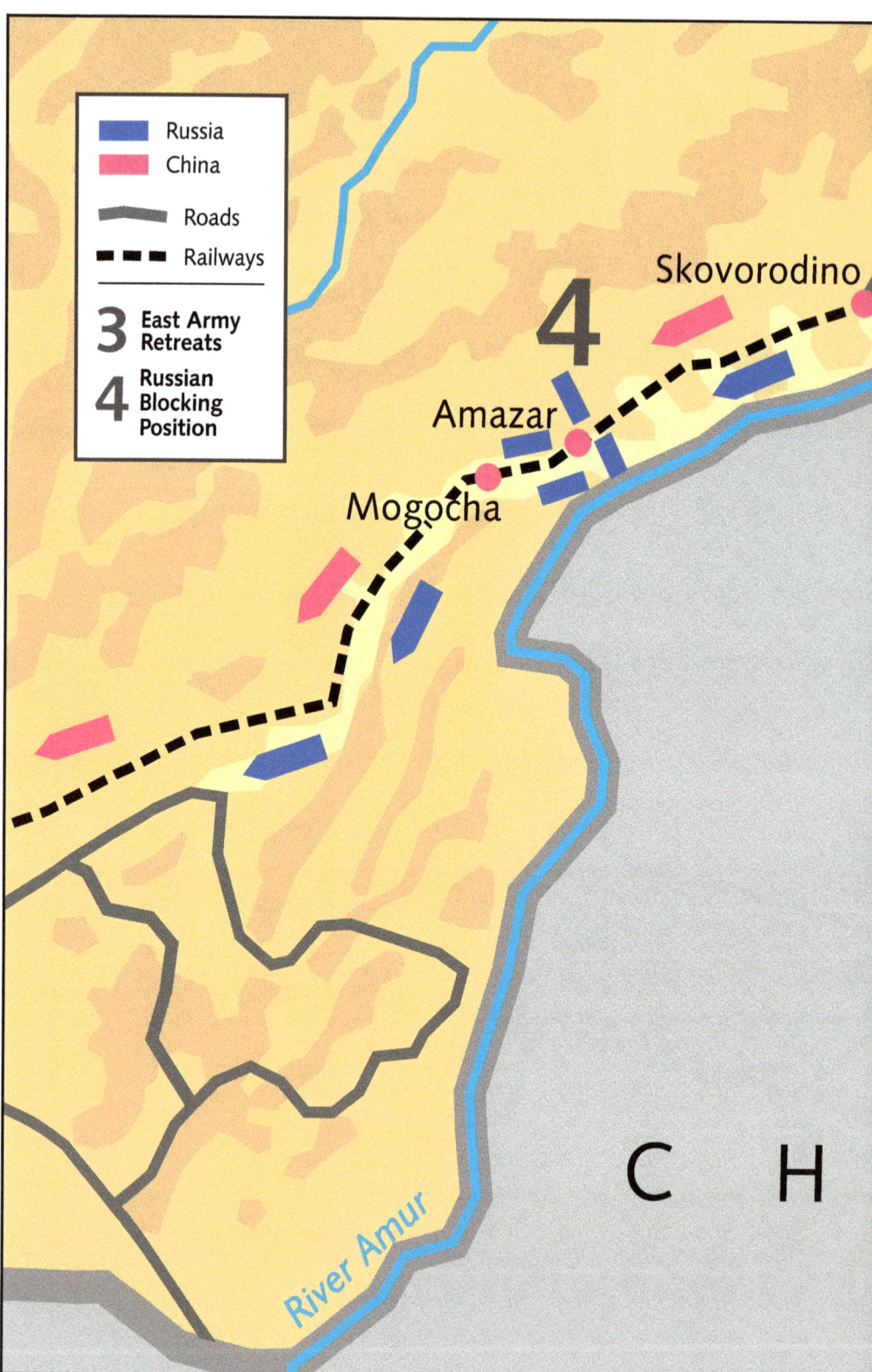

Russia
China
Roads
Railways
3 East Army Retreats
4 Russian Blocking Position

4

Skovorodino

Amazar

Mogocha

C H

River Amur

River Amur

Svobodnyy

Belogorsk

3

Blagoveshchensk

I   N   A

Russia
China
Roads
Railways

1 China invades
2 River Amur Held
3 East Army Retreats

3

Komsomolsk

River Amur

Khabarovsk

2

Birobidzhan

Vladivostok

CHINA

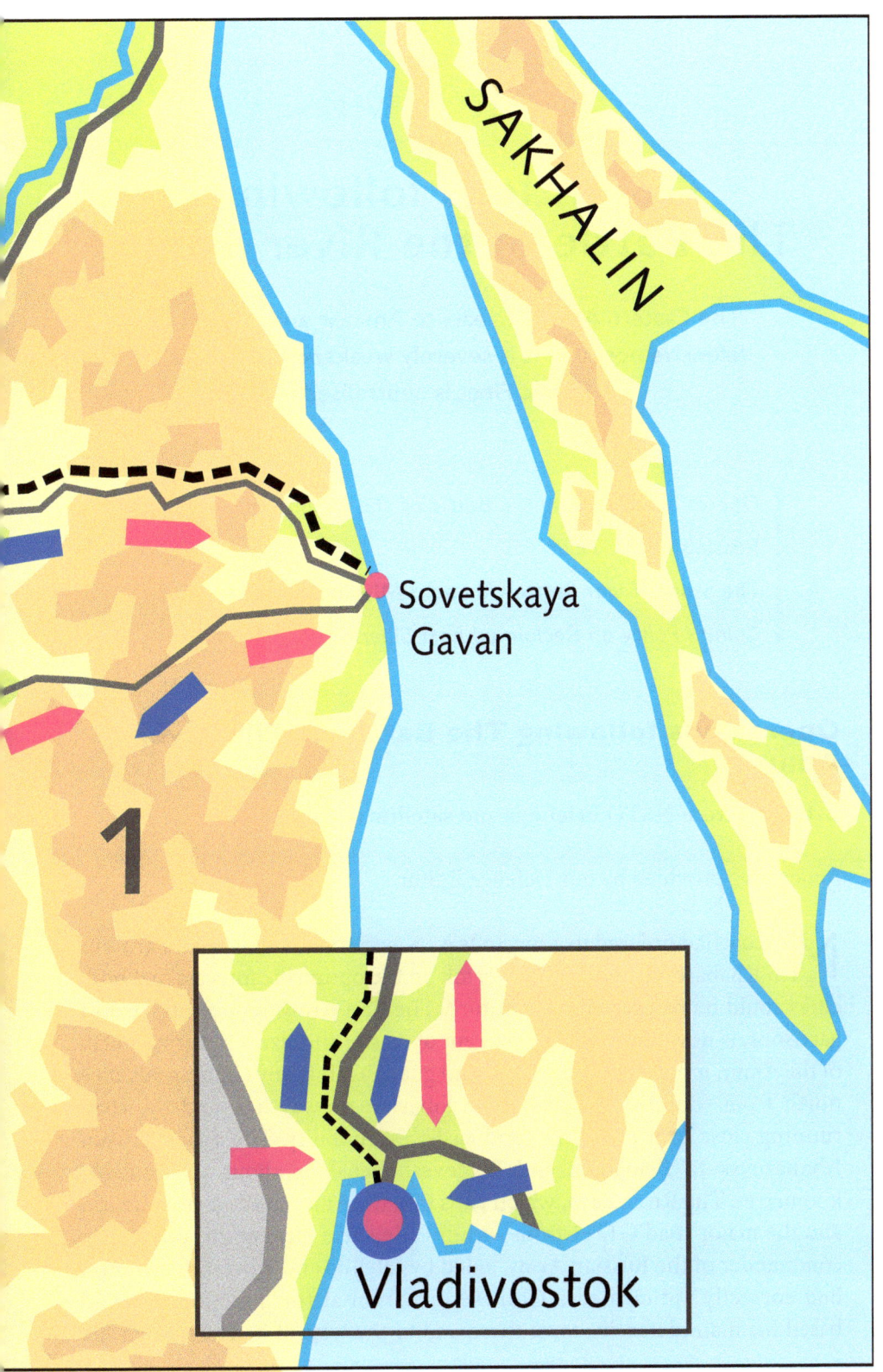

SAKHALIN

Sovetskaya
Gavan

1

Vladivostok

CHAPTER ELEVEN

Operations following The Battle of the River Amur

The Eastern Army retreats to Amazar and prepares a defensive position. It is severely weakened. The Russian Pacific Fleet is neutralised.

> *Operations Following the Battle of The River Amur*
>
> *Russia's Pacific Fleet*
>
> *The Story of Igor Statrov Aboad a Missile Launcher*
>
> *China's Policy on Reclaimed East Siberia*

Operations following The Battle of The River Amur

Extracted from NATO briefings and satellite images

A narrative provided by our Defence Editor

Moscow had ordered its army to leave a garrison of infantry and armour in Khabarovsk and in Vladivostok on the optimistic forecast that both cities could be recovered in the future. The East Army, reduced by its lost garrisons, is now down to sixty percent of its starting size. Operating north of the Amur, it now had to garrison and guard against any Chinese advance north from south of the river. The Siberian railway line and the road running close to it provided good east-west mobility. The distance from Khabarovsk to Belogorsk and Blagoveshchensk is about six hundred kilometres. The River Zeya, which runs into the Amur at Blagoveshchensk, and the major road G1211 from within China also meet at this point. The commander of the Russian Army, aided by satellite and air reconnaissance, had correctly anticipated a Chinese incursion at this junction and had based his main defensive force there and to the west of it. Thus, when the

Chinese successfully crossed the Amur there, the Russians were able to defend the position long enough for the bulk of the Russian Force to escape westward. By now, the Russian East Army was becoming disorganised. It was short of ammunition, fuel and food, and at least fifty percent of its armoured and wheeled strength had been lost through breakdown of old and poorly maintained equipment and ground and air attacks. The Army had not expected to operate for such a long period detached from its base, and logistic backup was inadequate. The East Army's task was now to protect, so far as possible, Russian territory to the north of the Amur whilst being aware of the Chinese advance towards it. It also had to take account of the excellent road system of the G202 running inside the Chinese border south of the Amur for about six hundred kilometres from Blagoveshchensk to Beijian.

West of the termination of the G202, the area between Amazar and Ignashino, both on the River Amazar, presented a reasonable defensive position with no through roads, open marshy country either side of the Siberian Railway and the river itself to cross. Defensive positions were set up along the River Amazar. Defence of this line would allow further defensive positions to be established to the west, either by the Russian West Army or NATO, if agreement with the latter was confirmed.

To the high command in Moscow, the situation looked bleak. The East Army was all but finished as a fighting force, and the West Army, still disengaging itself from Ukraine, was a long way from being able to reform and organise itself as a force able to confront the Chinese 'steamroller' approaching from the east.

Russia's Pacific Fleet

By our Defence Editor

During WWII, Russia's Pacific Fleet included up to eight hundred surface ships, made up of aircraft carriers (2), a battleship and a range of ships from cruisers to mine-clearance frigates and about one hundred and twenty submarines. With the fall of the USSR, Russia was unable to maintain such a large fleet, which by the mid-2020s had been reduced to: one cruiser, five destroyers, all reasonably modern, and up to twenty-five missile frigates which were now up to forty-five years old and no match for any western or Chinese units. By this time, China was able to assemble a fleet of more than three hundred and fifty modern units. In theory, Russia had plans to refurbish or replace its surface warships but had replaced very few. It did better in modernising its submarine fleet, including nuclear-propelled vessels fitted with long-range missiles and torpedoes. By the mid-2020s, the fleet consisted of six SSBN and SSK units in addition to a fleet of up to twenty diesel-powered older craft armed with torpedoes. The Pacific Fleet also included five to six brigades of naval infantry with amphibious and coastal defence responsibilities. Significant numbers of these infantry units were involved in Russia's war against Ukraine in 2022. The main base for the Pacific Fleet was Vladivostok, with smaller facilities in the north and around Kamchatka. At the time of the Chinese incursion into East Siberia, less than a third of the fleet's units were available for operations. The destruction of the cruiser Moskva in the Black Sea by a Ukrainian missile revealed the potential weaknesses of Russia's Pacific Fleet which, like the Moskva, was armed with deck-mounted cruise missiles. In western navies, the missiles are below decks in semi-protected silos. The missiles on Moskva were exposed to strikes by anything from a ship-mounted gun to air-delivered or land-based guided missiles. In the event, a single missile strike was sufficient to ignite one onboard missile, followed by the sympathetic detonation of others on deck. All structures above deck were cleared by the initial blast followed by conflagration within the hull, which suffered sufficient damage to cause the ship to sink. The missile carriers in the fleet were essentially unable to defend themselves. Confronted by Chinese naval units, those remaining at sea were sunk. Those still in port remained there and survived to be taken over by the Chinese Navy at leisure. The Chinese Navy then deployed a critical mass of submarine hunters to destroy any conventional submarines operating. The nuclear submarines were deployed further into the Pacific Ocean at the first signs of Chinese intent. The Russian Pacific Navy was no longer an effective fleet.

The Story of Igor Statrov – aboard Missile Launcher F585

Recorded by our Correspondent

> I saw the missile about three seconds before it hit the ship: a black object curving out of the clouds with fire and smoke roaring out of its tail. I had climbed out of the engine room to have a smoke and some fresh air. My head was just clear of the locker when I saw it. I saw trouble coming straight at me and

kept my head below the top of the locker as the blast, fire and smoke ripped over my head and over the stern of the ship. I felt the heat and choked on the smoke and fire which accompanied it. The blast only lasted a few seconds.

I looked up. The ship's bridge had disappeared, or at least most of it. Remnants of twisted steel, painted grey, with splashes of what was probably blood, hung over the sides of the ship. The missiles and their casings, located each side of the bridge, had disappeared, as had the 125mm gun and its armoured turret. The ship's deck had been cleared of all the paraphernalia of winches and lockers, and the forecastle was now a smoking hole. I saw all this within a few seconds of looking over the locker, which had protected me. I also noticed the smoke and flames were pouring out of the rocket ends of missiles in their tubes, forward of the bridge. The stairwell I had climbed was glowing beneath me. The interior of the ship appeared to be on fire. I heard shouts and cries for help from the engine room I had just left. They stopped very quickly. At that point, self-preservation prompted me to roll over the stern of the ship, landing in the water about three metres below.

The initial missile strike explosion had blown rubber life rafts off the deck and two were floating close to me. I am a non-swimmer; the presence of the life rafts saved my life. I climbed into the closest. My timing was fortunate. Above me, a new blast raised a plume of smoke above the ship. I assumed that one or more of our own missiles in their tubes had exploded. The ship was sinking anyway, as a consequence of the incoming missile strike, but the new terrifying explosion finished off the job. The hull seemed to rise in the air above me, slipped forward away from me and disappeared beneath the surface. From initial strike to finality had probably not taken more than two minutes. Alone in my raft, I appeared to be the only survivor.

Our flotilla had consisted of three ships. The nearest to me in my raft was about five hundred metres away. I began to wave, hoping for rescue, but my frantic efforts were brought to an end as I watched the last second or so of the flight path of a missile striking the bridge of my briefly perceived rescue ship. The sequence of events was as I had experienced only a few minutes earlier. The missile warhead struck just forward of the bridge. There must have been a large warhead in the missile, as the bridge disintegrated. It and the forward gun turret disappeared in a mass of flames and smoking scrap iron which went over the side. The sympathetic detonation of one of the ship's missiles occurred almost instantaneously as the prow of the ship heaved into the air and immediately began to sink. My rescuers probably did not need rescuing, as the ship sank so quickly. I assumed that all hands would have perished.

Enemy action appeared to have ceased. The one remaining ship of our flotilla searched the sea where our two ships had gone down and, finally, found me. I appear to have been quite lucky to have survived.

China's policy on reclaimed East Siberia

An extract from a statement issued by the Foreign Affairs Department of the Chinese Government

By our Beijing Correspondent

China has now recovered a significant area of territory ceded to Russia under the 'Unfair Treaty of Aigun'. Reunification of this land by military action was forced upon China consequent to Russia's refusal to enter into any negotiations. Now that reversal is in hand, the Chinese Government issues this preliminary statement on its policies relating to the recovered territory.

1. Repossession of the territory is irreversible.
2. Vladivostok and Khabarovsk are still held by Russian troops but surrounded by Chinese forces. It is assumed that they will eventually revert to Chinese control.
3. China will not follow the example of Russia displayed in Ukraine leading to massive destruction of property and mass civilian casualties. China will not support the beleaguered civilian and military personnel in any way but will encourage them to ultimately place their destiny in the hands of the Chinese state, given the assurance that they will not come to any harm.
4. China will wait for the Russian military forces involved to lay down

their arms and surrender to Chinese forces. China's policy will be to return them to Russian territory on conclusion of current hostilities. Prior to hostilities being forced on China, negotiations were held which included an offer by China to allow Russian nationals to remain on recovered land if they wished and were able to do so. However, all Russian state-owned land, including housing, will pass to Chinese ownership. China expects large numbers of Chinese citizens to migrate to recovered territory. Remaining Russians, if they so choose, will be treated with respect. This negotiating offer remains in place.

5. Any remaining Russian and other nationalities personnel will, over the space of twelve months, be repatriated to their own countries. Post war, a treaty will eventually be signed. The relevant sovereign nations concerned will compensate all their citizens for any harm or loss of assets consequent on wartime activities. China will not be held responsible for any compensation of Russian citizens.

6. All state and commercial assets will be acquired by the Chinese state without compensation.

7. China will not seek compensation from Russia for the losses and harm done by Russia to China's interests during the long period of unlawful occupation of Chinese territory.

8. China will continue its campaign against Russian forces until it has acquired sufficient territory to assure definable borders and to ensure that Russia can function efficiently within its newly defined borders and cannot, in future, present any economic, military or social threat to the Republic of China.

END OF STATEMENT

CHAPTER TWELVE

The Possibility of Nuclear War

The threat of a nuclear war launched by Russia is discounted. Mongolia, India, Japan and Pakistan express views and concerns. Japan occupies Sakhalin and the Kuril Islands.

The Possibility of Nuclear War

A Statement by Mongolia

A Statement by India

A Statement by Japan

Japanese Occupation of Sakhalin

The possibility of nuclear war: Russia/China

Prepared by our Defence Editor

At the time of Russia's invasion of Ukraine in 2022, the nuclear arsenals of the three major powers, including battlefield and strategic weapons, were approximately:

USA:	About 5,500
RUSSIA:	About 5,500
CHINA:	About 1,000

China had refrained from publicly showing its desire to overturn the Aigun Treaty terms, based upon the mistaken exaggeration of Russian military capability and also upon the known disparity between its own and Russia's nuclear arsenal. At this time, China has now created a position where nuclear first strike adequacy has been achieved. At the time of the conflict in Ukraine, the possibility of a war leading to nuclear conflict between the antagonists alarmed many within Russia and China and internationally. Given the overwhelming strength of China, the possibility of Russia reacting to potential defeat by using its nuclear capability was of great international concern. There is a good reason for this not to have taken place so far:

> The theory of 'mutual assured destruction' plays heavily on both parties to the conflict. Neither country wishes its heartland to be destroyed, and both powers are now in a position to achieve this if necessary, using their first striking capability.
>
> Within the Russian hierarchy, there were now many individuals who saw the course of action pursued by their leadership as indiscriminate, self-seeking and potentially destructive to the state of Russia itself. In particular, they were very troubled by the leadership's contention that the use of Russia's nuclear capability was the only option remaining to prevent overwhelming military defeat by China. They were aware that apart from collateral damage elsewhere in the world, the use of nuclear weapons would have internal consequences within Russia which would be catastrophic. The condition of Russia's ageing nuclear arsenal was also of concern. Comment has already been made that government expenditure on the armed services, based on a very meagre economy, had been less than adequate to maintain defences capable of sustaining internal and foreign policy objectives. This inadequacy applied equally to the maintenance of Russia's nuclear arsenal. Much of this had been manufactured in the period 1950–1975 to match the nuclear arsenal of the United States. Later additions tended to be of lower-yield battlefield weapons. All of it was now technically outdated and quite probably inadequately maintained. Even the military and technical experts charged with maintenance of the arsenal are probably reluctant to put it to use. They are concerned that rocket misfires are possible, causing local non-nuclear explosions, partial rocket firing causing low air burst explosions which would cause scattering of nuclear material over a wide area, or, worst of all, even local partial detonation of a nuclear warhead with widespread destruction on Russian territory. Under these conditions, initiating a nuclear conflict should be regarded by Russia as not acceptable. The Russian Government also had to remember that NATO also possessed overwhelming nuclear capability. The

consequences of a combined Chinese and NATO nuclear attack on Russia would cause unimaginable devastation, which should never be contemplated. The Russian Government in its present form, which had initiated policies leading to this impossible situation, should be removed, hopefully as a consequence of internal dissent.

A Press Statement: Issued by The Office of The President of Mongolia

By our Kyiv Correspondent

Mongolia has a high regard for its neighbours to the south (China) and the north (Russia). It very much regrets that both are now engaged in armed conflict, and Mongolia wishes to limit the potential harm which may come to it. The nation's armed forces are small compared to those of both our neighbours, but they will be deployed along our northern border to resist any incursion by the military of either side. We will remain steadfastly neutral in the current dispute and ask that our neighbours respect this position.

Comment by our Defence Correspondent

Mongolia has a population of about three and a half million spread over a very large country. Half of its people live in Ulan Bator. In the south is the Gobi Desert and the north consists of mountain ranges. China has, in the past, claimed Mongolia as part of Greater China, but a treaty agreed with Russia in 1921 confirmed its independence. Mongolia has, therefore, historical suspicions of any Chinese strategic plans which could affect its sovereignty. Its views on Russia are coloured by the help given in its war against the Japanese, when they controlled Manchuria in the 1930s, and also during World War II. It is likely that Mongolia will regard the gap between the mountain ranges south of Ulan-Ude and Lake Baikal and along the Trans-Mongolian Railway as weak points in its northern border. It appears to be planning a defensive position which will include a significant portion of its capability. Mongolian army equipment is old and obsolete, dating from the Soviet era, but is significant in total, including over one thousand tanks and other armoured vehicles, seven hundred artillery pieces and five hundred anti-aircraft items. It is certainly capable of mounting a determined defence in the limited area concerned. This will provide assurance to the NATO forces guarding the southern flank of the retreating Russian Army.

India's ongoing conflict with China and its effect on The China/Russia War

A paper prepared by our Defence Editor – China relations with other Asian countries

India

Northern borders: disagreements over the northern border between India and China were active in the days of the British Indian Empire. Some were settled amicably but others remained and cause ongoing hostilities between China and India.

Aksai Chin

China claims this large area as part of the Tibet Autonomous Region. It has built a road across it from Xinjiang to Tibet. India claims the area as part of Ladakh. A significant conflict between the two sides in 1967 and constant minor encounters sometimes involving artillery exchanges occur frequently.

Arunachal Pradesh

In the time of the British Raj this was called the North East Frontier Agency. China claims the whole Indian state as part of historical China, and both sides maintain military forces along the disputed frontiers; India deploys about two hundred and fifty thousand personnel and China about one hundred and twenty-five thousand. China has been accused of mounting border incursions then claiming territory as occupied as a form of 'salami slicing'.

Indian Ocean Region

Since independence in 1947, India has regarded its northern borders as possible sources of conflict. War with Pakistan in 1948, ongoing conflict with that country over Kashmir and conflict with China further reinforce this view. China's constant build-up of its naval power suggests imperial designs on the Pacific region in particular. China has also used its belt and braces strategy to secure agreements with the Maldives, Seychelles, the

Solomon Islands, Sri Lanka and Pakistan to secure naval facilities in addition to docking facilities in Djibouti. India recognises its limited military, economic and naval capability compared to China and seeks partnership with, for instance, Australia, Japan, France, the UK and the USA as a way of overcoming this. It has also considerably enhanced its diplomatic activity in the Indian Ocean Region (IOR) and beyond. It has established radar observation systems around the IOR. It sees the IOR as a maritime awareness domain and, with other countries, as a way of competing with China's belt and braces strategy. It holds naval exercises with its partners to reinforce its profile as the major power in the IOR.

Pakistan

Any event which increases Chinese pressure on Ladakh creates opportunity for Pakistan, which will take advantage if appropriate. Russian/Indian friendship is long-standing. India will support Russia should the need arise. Pakistan is a Muslim state following Sharia law and a leader of the Muslim world. A nuclear power with large armed forces of over a million personnel. Pakistan has close relations with China and with Iran and Turkey. It is not an ally of NATO or the USA but does assist both in countering terrorism, with operations in the north-west frontier region against Taliban and Muslim extremists. Its main foreign engagement is with India, which claims the whole of Jammu and Kashmir. Control is currently shared; there have been three wars over the territory and relations are always tense. Pakistan helped resist the Russian occupation of Afghanistan. Pakistan is a major ally of China which supports it in its quarrel with India, and China is a major importer of Pakistan's exports. Pakistan is reliant on China for political and military support against India should the need arise. Pakistan will support China if appropriate in its fight with Russia.

Japan relates to The China/Russia conflict

From our Tokyo Correspondent – a press release

The Japanese Cabinet met yesterday. It was a routine weekly meeting normally only reported on if anything unusual justified the issue of a press statement. On this occasion, it did. A major item for discussion was the current position in relation to the Japanese sovereignty of the Kuril Islands. The Cabinet noted the statement from Chinese sources that the Chinese

Politburo had discussed the dispute which now existed between China and Russia in connection with the Aigun Treaty. The People's Daily – which answers to the Chinese Communist Party – is now leading a narrative discussion on the rights and wrongs of the treaty, with the emphasis being on the wrong done to China by Russia in annexing such a large area of Chinese territory, and why the time has now come to reclaim the land. Whilst copy in the *People's Daily* would reflect opinions in the higher reaches of the Communist Party, its semi-official nature and in the absence of a government statement, the narrative could be disclaimed as being not official policy. However, less prestigious local newspapers and social media indicate that discussion of the Aigun Treaty is now beginning to be a major subject of interest to the Chinese population generally.

The Japanese Cabinet received a briefing on the implications for Japanese foreign policy given the proximity of the territories in question to Japan. The Cabinet was briefed on the history of Sakhalin and the Kuril Islands. Japan first laid claim to Sakhalin in 1805 together with the Kuril Islands, which connect it to Japan's mainland. Sakhalin was partitioned with Russia throughout the 19th century, a share formalised in 1905 consequent on the Russia/Japan war. This confirmed partition, with Russia retaining North Sakhalin and with Japan confirming ownership of the south, together with the Kuril Islands. The Cabinet was reminded that the whole of this territory was then seized by Russia at the very end of the Second World War, and after Japan's surrender. Ownership by Russia of these territories has never been formally agreed. Japan has, on a number of occasions, asked for the return of the southern Kuril Islands but Russia has refused to negotiate. Japan continues to insist that the south of Sakhalin and the whole of the Kuril Islands are historical Japanese territories and their seizure by Russia is equivalent to the unequal Treaty of Aigun. Japan takes great interest in any conversations between China and Russia on these issues, and will continue to claim sovereignty over Sakhalin and the Kurils.

Japanese occupation of Sakhalin

From the Tokyo Correspondent

It is reported that Japanese army and marine troops have landed in Aniva Bay, close to the capital city, Yuzhno-Sakhalinsk. They were supported by aircraft flying from the Japanese island Hokkaido and by a navy escort fleet. The Russian garrison had already been withdrawn and Chinese troops now occupied the whole of the Siberia Pacific coastline. Given the proximity of Chinese forces to Sakhalin, it is assumed that China and Japan have reached agreement to allow the Japanese occupation. The Chinese will have calculated that Japan, given the collapse of Russian control, would be vigorous in claiming the Sakhalin and the Kurils, and, as neither had ever been in Chinese hands, it was therefore prepared to allow Japan to take control rather than have a hostile Japan to its east as it fought the Russians to its west.

CHAPTER THIRTEEN

The Assassination of the Russian President

The President decrees further mobilisation. The President is assassinated and the Defence Minister and Military Chief of Staff are arrested.

Russia Mobilises Additional Reserves

Formal Notice: Death of the President of Russia

Russian Security Council Meeting

Russia mobilises additional reserves

A report by our Moscow Correspondent

I am standing in Red Square. Overnight, the Kremlin announced that it was mobilising reserves as reinforcements for its army, fighting in Ukraine. It also announced that up to 10% of FSB and Ministry of Internal Affairs personnel are to be formed into units capable of being deployed in offensive operations in Ukraine. During the last mass mobilisation of about three hundred thousand men, which took place in September of 2022, these police units were not included. The personnel concerned will not be happy about this. It is nine am, cold and wet, but I am not alone. The last mobilisation event drew tens of thousands of protesters onto the square; I anticipate many more this time. The President, be it as president or prime minister, has been in power for many years. In that time, he has hollowed out the democratic heart of the state and replaced it with an increasingly authoritarian regime, oppressing free speech and incarcerating journalists and anyone brave enough to question his legitimacy and actions. The understood but unstated contract between him and his subjects was that they were content to allow him to exercise strong government, so long as their lives improved socially and financially in a secure environment. Initially, the 'Special Military Operation' was taken at face value as necessary and justified. The first mobilisation punctured this cosy system and caused wild alarm in the population, troubled by the prospect of a conflict impinging on their lives. More than one hundred thousand expressed their alarm, sensing that they would be affected, by leaving Russia. Many were young and highly trained and a positive loss to the state. This new mobilisation really has caused alarm. The Russian people have become aware through social media that the Russian Army is not living up to the victorious image presented by state propaganda and is especially aware of the high human cost to its soldiers, measured by the body bags frequently pictured on social media. Their alarm has been reinforced by the news that erstwhile Chinese allies are now causing trouble in Siberia. Propaganda has played down this problem and the Russian people are typically very loyal to their land and state, but obviously further mobilisation of military reservists for service in Ukraine, a war which most Russians see as uncalled-for, and the new threat from China have raised a cacophony of alarm bells in the people of Moscow, and throughout Russia. They are now genuinely alarmed that their personal and national security is at risk.

The square has now filled with a multitude of a size which dwarfs anything I have seen before. The crowd is bigger than my ability to count: a million? What is certain is that it is now beyond the capacity of the law enforcement presence to handle. There are plenty of police but they are standing back on the periphery of the crowd, making no arrests and, if anything, adding to the feeling of revolution in the air. Perhaps they see themselves being marched off to Ukraine. The state has now lost control of the situation. There is no way in which this mobilisation is going to be permitted by the population. My personal view is reinforced by news I am getting from cities in European Russia and Siberia that recruitment offices and some government buildings have been burnt down. This vast crowd is not going to be dispersed anytime soon and is becoming more vocal and hostile as time goes by. Placards in effect shouting for the President of Russia to go are now everywhere. The President has lost the support of his people. It remains to be seen what the governing system around him will do.

Formal Notice

Death of The President of Russia

The following statement was made on all television channels with the simultaneous release of a press statement

By our Moscow Correspondent

It is with extreme regret that the Russian Government announces the death of the President of Russia. His Defence Minister and the Chief of the General Staff have both been arrested. In the absence of a vice-president, and until the appointment of a new president, the Prime Minster will continue to run the Government with enhanced responsibilities and with the full support of the General Staff. A new chief of the general staff will be announced shortly. The nation will share a day of mourning at the end of this month so that the population may express its regret and its appreciation of the valuable service which the President has performed on behalf of the nation.

The President of Russia Assassinated (1)

Information obtained from Russian state TV programme

By our Moscow Correspondent

This news has been announced by Russian TV news channels. It has not yet been corroborated, but such an announcement and its source indicate that there must be a significant element of truth in a story which would not have been allowed to air without very senior authorisation. In some respects, this is an unsurprising event, given the increasingly bad (from the Russian President's point of view) scenario which has emerged from Moscow in the past week. News of the continuing advance of Chinese forces in the east, of upheaval in Ukraine and of massive anti-war demonstrations in Moscow, St Petersburg and almost all Russian cities has led to a sense of panic amongst all Russian politicians and bureaucrats which has been communicated to western news agencies and politicians. The newsflash ended with an anticipated statement that everything was under control within the government, that the people were asked to stay calm and that further announcements would be made very quickly. There was conjecture as to who or what will take charge. Government authority was very concentrated in the Russian President's hands. There is no vice-president, and the prime minister plays a very minor part in the process of government seen by the outside world. The military heads of the three services are currently very much in the news given the vulnerable strategic military position in which Russia now finds itself. The Russian Security Council had previously been called upon to give support to the President's position whilst he had struggled to control events. Further information will be published as it becomes available.

The Death of The President of Russia – Russian Security Council Meeting

From our Correspondent in Moscow

The Security Council had planned to meet on this day to discuss the situation in Ukraine and in eastern Siberia. This purpose has now been compounded by the need to assess the popular reaction to the announcement of a further round of mobilisation and how to deal with this.

There has been no official release of the details surrounding the Russian President's death, but information is emerging via briefings to officials and friends of members of the Russian Security Council, which was meeting when the event occurred.

As was customary, the President sat alone facing his council with each member in turn walking to a podium to address him and his fellow councillors. It was the turn of the head of the FSB, the Russian Secret Service. He walked to the podium and took out from the file he was carrying what looked like a thick pen. He walked towards the Russian President, stood before him, raised the pen, which turned out to be a pistol, and shot him in the forehead. James Bond could not have done any better. What was then surprising was that there was some clapping from some of the councillors. Normally frightened by the overbearing president, they suddenly found themselves free from the threat he represented and realised that there was now a possible way out of the disastrous situation which he had created.

Immediately after the pistol shot was heard, a unit of FSB Spetsnaz heavily armed soldiers entered the room. Four of the soldiers marched up to the defence minister and chief of the general staff, forced them to their feet and marched them out of the room. The remaining detachment stayed behind their leader. This quietened down the room activity and allowed the FSB head to speak:

"We all realise and are very concerned about the geopolitical position in which Russia now finds itself. The President's adventure in Ukraine has proved to be a major strategic error. He expected his troops to be greeted as welcomed saviours. Instead, they were immediately confronted with a very hostile population and military, leading to a violent war which we appear to be unable to win. Ukraine has gained the support of the EU and NATO, which raises the very likely possibility that we will have NATO troops on our eastern border. This position is compounded by the decisions of Sweden and Finland to join the alliance. Our western border is more exposed to hostile intent than it has ever been.

"The Russian President's refusal to discuss East Siberia with China has led to us losing that territory irredeemably whilst creating another border to defend, with constantly diminishing means. I am sure that some agreement could have been reached with China which would have allowed Russia to retain at least a significant presence in Siberia. Our resources, economic and military, have been reduced to the point where it is not impossible for us to contemplate the total subjugation of Russia for the first time since the Mongols caused so much damage in the thirteenth and fourteenth centuries. It seems to me that we must now sue for peace and find friends wherever possible. I therefore propose that we now act together to decide that:

1. You agree my diagnosis of the present situation.
2. We elect a new leader as president who will be acceptable to all of us, to the population in general and to current NATO protagonists whom we may now look to as potential saviours. I suggest that the role of interim president should be assumed by the new chief of the general staff. We will confirm his appointment and presidential role at the next meeting of the Security Council which will be held within the next forty-eight hours. His role as interim president will be held until the next presidential election. That is the reality of the situation.
3. We recognise our European roots, profess to return to them and seek assistance from the EU and NATO to prevent any further intrusion onto our land by Chinese forces. I propose an approach through a diplomatic route to the EU and NATO to achieve this aim.

4. Our very first task must be to control the popular insurrection
    which is taking place in the streets of Moscow and throughout
    Russia. We must clearly state that stability on the streets must be
    reinstated, by force if necessary, but also that the fears of our people
    must be recognised and assuaged by the broadcasting of the steps
    we are about to take.

The meeting collectively agreed these proposals.

CHAPTER FOURTEEN

The Involvement of The EU and NATO

Russia seeks assistance from the EU/NATO to help contain China's advance. After two meetings of foreign ministers, Russia is forced to agree EU/NATO terms including relinquishment of territory illegally seized by Russia before and after WWII.

Russia/NATO Negotiations

Russia Seeks NATO's Help

Meeting of EU Foreign Ministers and SHAPE

Russian Predatory Annexations

Russia and NATO Negotiations

From our Correspondent attending the talks held at NATO HQ

The first meeting between NATO and Russia was held at a political level between a deputation of foreign ministers, including the NATO Secretary General and members of its Governing Council, and the Chief of the Russian General Staff. The meeting was an abrasive display of petulance from the Russian delegation, humiliated by the need to be seeking succour from its erstwhile enemy and grandiloquently producing a list of demands in an attempt to remain in control, so far as it could, of its destiny. Russian demands included a requirement that a Russian commander be appointed as head of the joint Russian/NATO force to confront the Chinese Army. This request was firmly rejected by NATO, which insisted that NATO's supreme commander in Europe would head the force. The Russian delegation also presented a list of demands limiting the responsibilities and political control of NATO forces acting without Russia's approval. All these demands were rejected by the NATO delegation. At this point, the Russian delegation complained that they were being treated as supplicants, which they were, and left the meeting in high umbrage. No later meeting was arranged.

A Summary of The Position which led Russia to Seek NATO'S Help

By our Defence Correspondent

With the death of the Russian President, and related arrests, the General Staff under a new commander has now taken control of the Russian Government. Under its new interim president, the chief of the general staff, its current main concern is the constant progress of Chinese forces from the east. Russia now has no friends of any consequence and the General Staff considers that, in the end, it may have to sue for peace with China and accept the loss of face, autonomy, economic well-being and its position as an erstwhile superpower. Its possession of the world's largest nuclear stockpile could protect it from catastrophic destruction, but its use now, when China has reached an adequate equivalence in nuclear yield, does not present itself as an option. The position Russia now finds itself in is blamed on the strategic mistakes made in the latter years of the President's administration. In the west, it created a permanently hostile state in the form of Ukraine, which fought a debilitating war against the Russian invader, and left a hostile population and an ongoing guerrilla war which requires the attention of a third of the Russian Army to contain. NATO was rejuvenated and expanded by its opposition to that war, and in Russia the economy suffered under the economic straitjacket imposed on it by the west generally and a large portion of the world's governments. Finally, the damage caused by the Ukraine Army, including military losses in the initial conflict and the ongoing military commitment, coupled with the severe loss of economic output and the privations of Russian civil society, display evident weaknesses in the overall ability of the Russian state to protect itself.

This has led the Chinese state, with renewed forcefulness, to refer to what it has always called the unfair Aigun Treaty of 1858. The coincident unfair treaties which created British Hong Kong and Portuguese Macau were corrected in the late 20th century, but the loss of over one million square kilometres of land, along the Pacific coastline to Russia, has remained a brooding problem within China's governing class. China had stayed its hand in the 20th century given Russia's massive nuclear capability and original comparative economic strength compared with that of China. Times have changed; China's economy is now ten times the size of Russia's. Its population is ten times the size and its armed forces are larger and much better equipped. In the course of the Russia/Ukraine war, China has reached adequate nuclear parity with Russia. China is strong and Russia is weak. The President of Russia was not prepared to recognise this disparity and even less inclined to contemplate any loss of territory in eastern Siberia. He refused to discuss the issue, refused to contemplate and compromise, and resolutely held to the view that Russia could contain China. Finally, the call for a nuclear alert during the Ukraine War was regarded by the General Staff as an unnecessary and dangerous move which might have initiated a nuclear war with NATO. Thus, the General Staff considers that Russia's strategic position has become unstable. It needs massive assistance to even ensure its survival. Friendless Russia very badly needed friends, and the only power able to affect this issue was NATO, including its largest constituent, the United States of America. This was a shocking realisation for the erstwhile superpower and competitor of the United States, but no other option appeared to be available and the General Staff, representing the Russian Government, reconciled itself to the fait accompli and agreed to approach NATO and seek its help.

Meeting of EU Member States' Foreign Ministers. Also Present: USA, UK, The NATO Secretary General and Commander of SHAPE: Supreme Headquarters Allied Powers Europe

The following communication was issued after the meeting, which was held to discuss the ongoing Russian/Chinese war

By our Correspondent

Russia is a European country. It has suffered intrusion from the West, including invasion by Napoleon, the attack on Crimea by Britain and France and the savage attack by Hitler. However, in more recent times, Russia, in its turn, has attempted to subvert western democracies from the time of the Russian Revolution in 1917 through Stalin and by the invasion of Ukraine in 2022. Now it finds itself in dire straits as a consequence of attack from the East by China. It has formally requested assistance from the EU and NATO and associated friendly countries to repel the Chinese attack.

Western Europe, represented here primarily by the EU, cannot ignore the threat to Russia's very existence and the consequent potential threat to the democracies represented here. We have therefore determined to mount collective action to support Russia and help defend it against the Chinese threat. The collective action to be taken will be outlined in a meeting between the EU, NATO and the Russian Government, which will be held very quickly. However, it is a requirement that any support from the EU/NATO will depend upon Russia correcting numerous irregular territorial acquisitions made by it since 1945. Agreement by the Russian Government to the actions we propose below is necessary before collective support can be provided.

The Russian Government is to agree to the following:

1. The terms of the Treaty of Aigun of 1858 were forced upon a weak Chinese government unable to resist the military might of Imperial Russia. At that time, other treaties were forced upon China by Europe, including the annexation of Hong Kong and Macau, and trade rights given to other European powers. The unfair treaties and trading rights referred to were reversed in the twentieth and twenty-first centuries, except for the Treaty of Aigun. The Russian Government must now accept the reversal of the terms of that treaty. The EU accepts the right of China to recover all the land lost to the east of the Ussuri River and north of the River Amur, west to the original western boundary and other land bordering it, over which it historically claimed sovereignty. This area is ill defined and will be the subject of negotiation between interested powers under the auspices of the United Nations and, in particular, under the control of the Security Council, without the participation of Russia and China, and working with the Secretary General of the UN, who will chair the planning sessions of the Council and who, in conjunction with the Security Council and UN General Assembly, will make the final judgement of the boundary issues concerned. These agreed boundaries will be subject to a simple majority vote by the members of the General Assembly.
2. The Russian Government accepts that its new international boundary will be to the east of the Ural Mountains, laying on the 70° parallel to the eastern shores of the Kara Sea in the north and Omsk in the south.

3. It will accept that the land east of 70° longtitude as far as the boundaries of Buryatia and the east shore of Lake Baikal – which it is anticipated will be a new western boundary of China – will become a new federal country, becoming the homeland of the ethnic groups who were its original inhabitants until banished by the eastward expansion by Russia, and the Sibiriaks, who have since settled there.

4. The following section lists and maps territories annexed by Russia as a consequence of occupation by Russian armies from 1860 to the present. Prior occupation by Russian troops led the West to acquiesce in the annexations, but current circumstances allow the annexations to be reversed if practical. The Russian Government will accept the transfer of territory back to the original nations, as detailed in the following paragraphs. In general, the transfers must be carried out with the majority agreement of existing populations. Referenda will need to be held. These will be supervised by the EU and the results and consequences reported to the Security Council and General Assembly of the UN; the result of referenda will not be challenged by the Russian Government.

Russian Predatory Annexations

Russia has been a predatory nation since the early expansion of the Muscovy state from the 1500s onwards. Annexations in more recent times related to this narrative can be grouped as follows:

Historic

The outcome of various campaigns in the Caucasus in the nineteenth century led to the annexation and absorption into the Russian Empire of:

Dagestan, Chechnya and Ingushetia

Each of these countries, although formally part of the Russian state, include robust independence movements and should now achieve freedom and statehood.

Linked to World War II

At the end of WWII, Russia controlled the whole of eastern Europe. At the Yalta Conference, the two other major allied powers (the USA and UK) which had fought Hitler agreed, with little choice, to adjust East European borders. These suited Russia's social, economic and military objectives, including major changes in national boundaries and population movements. It was also agreed that other territory on Russia's own borders could be incorporated into Russia. After seventy-three years of status quo, it would now be impractical to reverse many of these changes. These situations are listed below. However, it was considered that changes occurring in Russia's own borders should be reversed. In particular, the following territories should be returned to the parent nation:

Kaliningrad	:	to Lithuania or Poland (originally German)
Transnistria	:	to Moldova
Sakhalin and the Kuril Islands	:	to Japan
Abskasia and South Ossetia	:	to Georgia
Karelia	:	to Finland
Donbas, Southern Ukraine and Crimea	:	to Ukraine

Border Changes to Remain

Border changes imposed following Yalta should now remain unchanged. Nations affected are:

Germany
Poland
Hungary
Romania
Ukraine

The Baltic Nations

The major issue concerning the Baltic states is the mass immigration of Russian citizens into the states, forced on them by Russia post-1945. The states concerned, given the collapse of the Russian state, are now exercising their authority over the immigrants to ensure that they either accept the nationality of the host states and integrate into them or return to Russia. No further action is required.

Maps on the following pages show the areas mentioned above.

GERMAN TERRITORIAL LOSSES 1919/1945

DENMARK
SWEDEN

North Sea

Baltic Sea

Memel to Lithuania 1923

North Schleswig to Denmark 1919

Danzig

KALININGRAD

Hanburg

NETHERLANDS

Berlin

East Prussia to Russia (Kaliningrad) and Poland 1945

West Prussia to Poland 1919

GERMANY

BELGIUM

Eupen-Maimedy to Belgium 1919

Frankfurt

Posen to Poland 1919

POLAND

LUX

Alsace Lorraine to France 1919

Pomerania & Silesia to Poland 1945

Upper Silesia to Poland 1922

CZECH REPUBLIC

FRANCE

Stuttgart

Hlucin Region to Czechoslovakia 1920

SLOVAKIA

Munich

AUSTRIA

HUNGARY

SWITZERLAND

0   50   100 miles

Territory annexed by Russia   Borders set by Russia

Germany lost very large areas of territory in 1945, largely to Poland.
Reversal of these changes and population movements are not now practical.

KALININGRAD

Territory annexed by Russia

Kaliningrad was annexed in1945 from Poland and Lithuania to Russian, so should be returned. Russian settlers should integrate or return to Russia.

POLAND TERRITORIAL LOSSES AND GAINS 1945

Territory annexed by Russia **Borders set by Russia**

Large areas of Polish Territory were annexed to Russia in 1945, aquired by Belarus and Ukraine. Population movement is now inpractical. The same applies to areas of East Germany around the river Oder and south of Danzig gained by Poland

POST WW2 PARTITION OF HUNGARY

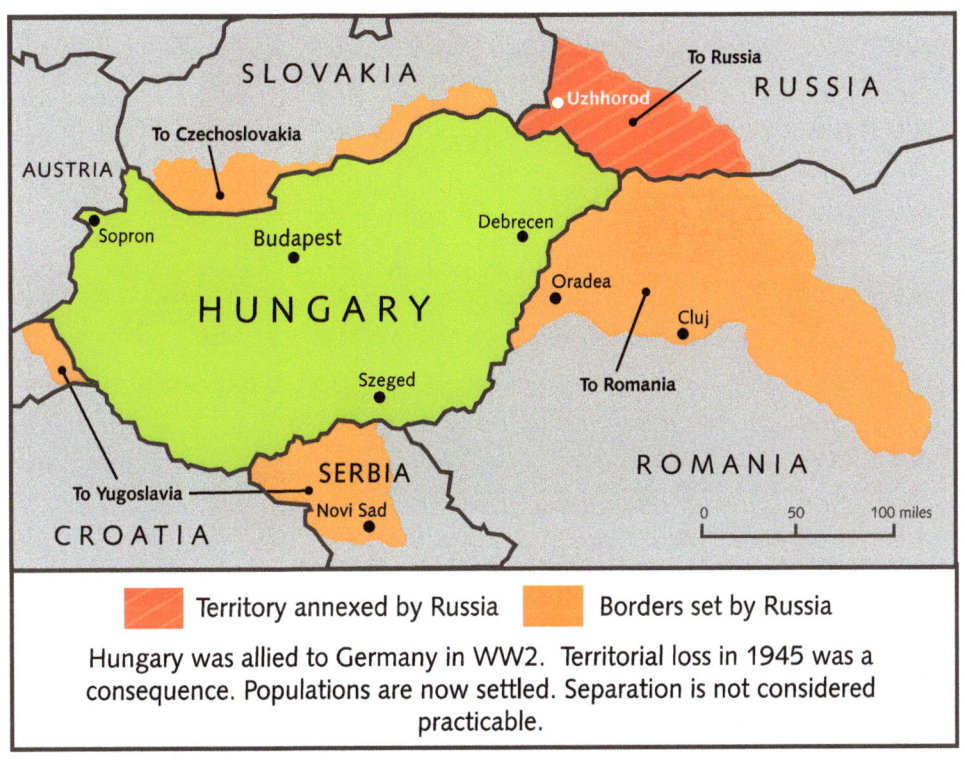

SLOVAKIA

To Russia

RUSSIA

Uzhhorod

To Czechoslovakia

AUSTRIA

Sopron

Budapest

Debrecen

HUNGARY

Oradea

Cluj

Szeged

To Romania

SERBIA

ROMANIA

To Yugoslavia

Novi Sad

CROATIA

0   50   100 miles

Territory annexed by Russia   Borders set by Russia

Hungary was allied to Germany in WW2. Territorial loss in 1945 was a
consequence. Populations are now settled. Separation is not considered
practicable.

ROMANIA

UKRAINE

To Russia 1940

MOLDOVA

HUNGARY

Odessa

ROMANIA

Bucharest

SERBIA

Black
Sea

0   50   100 miles

BULGARIA   To Bulgaria

Territory annexed by Russia   Borders set by Russia

Romania joined Germany in its assault on Russia but joined the western forces
in the later stages of the war. Russia annexed part of Romania in 1945.
The annexed portion is now part of Ukraine. Population movements took
place but separation is not practicable.

MOLDOVA AND TRANSNISTRIA

Territory annexed by Russia

Moldova was administered by Russia between 1812 and 1917, then by Romania until it was regained by Russia between 1940 and 1990, when it gained its independence.

Transnistria is part of Moldova. Russian inspired unrest in its North East lead to a break away statelet, now occupied by Russian Troops. They should be removed allowing Moldova to reclaim its territory.

FINLAND AFTER 1945

Karelia, Salla and Petsamo were annexed by Russia at the end of 1945 and should be returned to Finland. Russian settlers should integrate or return to Russia.

TERRITORIAL CHANGES OF THE BALTIC STATES 1939 - 1945

0   50   100 miles

Gulf of Finland

Baltic Sea

Tallinn

Narva

ESTONIA

Area transferred to Russia in November 1944

Lake Peipus

RUSSIA

Gulf of Riga

Area transferred to Russia in August 1944

Area transferred to Russia in August 1944

Riga

LATVIA

Part of Lithuania 1923 -1939 ceded to Germany in March 1939. Returned to Lithuania in 1945

LITHUANIA

Vilnius transferred to Lithuania in November 1945

Vilnius

BELARUS

RUSSIA

Kaliningrad

Transferred to Lithuania in November 1940

POLAND

■ Territory annexed by Russia   ■ Borders set by Russia

Further areas of the Baltic States were annexed to Russia in 1945 (See Kaliningrad).

UKRAINE WAR - SITUATION AT 28TH FEBRUARY 2023

BELARUS

RUSSIA

Chernobyl

Sumy

Kyiv

UKRAINE

Kharkiv

Kupyansk

Svatove

Izyum

Kreminna

Slovyansk

Soledar

Luhansk

Klishchiivka

Bakhumut

Dnipro

Avdiivka

Kryvyi Rih

Zaporizhzhya

Donetsk

MOLDOVA

Mariupol

Melitopol

Kherson

Odesa

Azov Sea

CRIMEA

RUSSIA

Black Sea

0   50   100 miles

Ukraine territory held by Russia

Regained by Ukraine

THE CAUCASUS

Ten countries/tribal groups are currently Republics within the Russian Federation but seek independence. Ethnic population have become a minority. Russian settlers should either integrate or return to Russia. Russia maintains 3,000 troops in Armenia and is reluctant to remove them.

GEORGIA

| Territory annexed by Russia | Borders set by Russia |

Pro Russian settlers claimed Abkhazia and South Ossetia and annexed them with the help of Russian troops. Both areas should be reintegrated into Georgia.

MANCHURIA - RUSSIA BOUNDARY

Land annexed by Russia from China
1858, Treaty of Aigun   1860, Peaking Conference

SAKHALIN AND KURIL ISLANDS

Territory annexed by Russia

The south of the island of Sakhalin and the Kuril Islands were occupied in the closing days of WW2 by Russia which has refused to return them.

CHAPTER FIFTEEN

The Interest of the United States of America in Siberia

The USA State of Alaska is only 85 kilometres from Siberia. The USA will react strongly against any threat to that state but in principle supports China's wish to recover land lost to Russia in Siberia.

The USA in Eastern Siberia – A China Forward Paper

A USA State Department Briefing

The Interest of The United States in Eastern Siberia

A paper by China Forward: press release

We have written extensively on that part of north-east Siberia which is, historically, Chinese territory, lost to Russia by the unfair Treaty of Aigun of 1858/60. We have recommended that China now takes steps to recover that land. We are persuaded to take this position by the recent Russian loss of authority and economic and military capability as a consequence of its failed attempt to restore some of its lost glory by occupying Ukraine. The USA clearly has a very strong interest in Russia's current and future position and will react to anything which could affect that interest to its disadvantage. The acquisition by China of territory in east and north Siberia falls into this category. China cannot make any dramatic moves in that area without considering the reaction of the USA and taking steps to modify that reaction in its favour. The current geopolitical position is that the USA is in a confrontational situation, through NATO, on Russia's western border but could, extraordinarily, move into a position of cooperation with Russia on its eastern border if China made any aggressive moves in that area with which the USA disagreed. This paper addresses the current situation and poses a way ahead which would satisfy both the USA and China.

The first principle of any potential agreement over the way ahead is that both countries have to recognise that the remaining superpowers, including India, must, in their mutual interests, cooperate on the world stage. The world and its populations would be severely damaged as a consequence of military clashes. We suggest that three superpowers recognise the implicit existence of their own spheres of interest and recognise those of the other two in order to remove reasons for confrontation. Their interest must be actually and recognisably benign and organised as military blocs only as an obvious form of self-defence.

This situation relegates significant but lesser powers to a secondary role, which they might find embarrassing but necessary in their own long-term interests. In order to address the possibility of agreeing spheres of interest, it is necessary to discuss areas of contention which need to be resolved.

Political Ideology

In the 1960s, China set out to build an economy based on the capitalist system developed in Europe and USA. It based its model on state enterprises in the older engineering and labour-intensive industries but also persuaded major western technology companies to base production facilities in China, in return for access to their intellectual property, given the promise of a very large potential market. Having established its own technological industrial base, China now shows signs of reverting, in part, to the traditional communist state control. This approach may create harm in the future but, for the moment, the country's economy is robust and reliant upon the combined system of capitalist and state control which it has created. China's state system and the capitalist system of the USA should be able to operate in competitive but harmonious duality. Both will compete, especially in developing countries, but that should not lead to conflict. Thus, they create their own spheres of influence whose stability is beneficial to both and should lead to increased prosperity throughout the world. We need to look at the areas where harmony is less evident. The major point of conflict is in the South China Sea, which China essentially claims as its own territorial water, and especially Taiwan, the home of the Kuomintang. The USA has, more or less, promised to come to its aid if China attempts to annex what is a flourishing independent nation. This potential conflict has to be decided harmoniously. Currently, no discussions are taking place between China and the USA. At the moment, the prospect of agreement seems remote but at some stage this must surely be reached. The Taiwanese could be content to accept some form of federal structure, and the USA would certainly be relieved to remove this potential hot spot from its problem list. The USA and China should meet to discuss this issue and, hopefully, resolve it. Taiwan is a major but not the only South China Sea problem causing friction. China's claim, outlined in the nine-dash claim to most of the sea, impinges on the territorial waters of the dozen or so countries on its periphery. China has created the possibility of conflict by creating militarised bases built on uninhabited rocks and islands, causing great concern to those same peripheral countries. The USA support of freedom of navigation through the South China Sea creates confrontation between China and the USA, which could lead to a major military conflict. This paper can offer no particular solution to a problem which has been created by China. Some concessions to and by China are likely to be required to lessen China's threat to its neighbours, probably by sharing sovereignty over these bases. Concessions by China could probably be rewarded by the USA looking more favourably on its acquisition of territory in Siberia. The balance of concessions should also include other areas in which competitive conflict is possible.

The other potential superpower is India, with which conflict with China already exists involving their shared border in the Himalayas and especially in Ladakh. This area has for many years been the scene of numerous border incidents, leading to clashes and loss of life. At present, China occupies a large area of seized Indian land. China also has a long-held claim to the Indian state of Uttar Pradesh. Further antagonism is caused by China's occupation of Tibet, not recognised by India, which continues to host the Dalai Lama, and also by Chinese support given to Pakistan over the latter's claim to Kashmir. India could be invited to support China's claims in Siberia in exchange for settlement of outstanding issues in Ladakh, Uttar Pradesh and Nepal.

China would not be well served by a clash that could involve itself, India and Pakistan in that region. This is especially so given the growingly fractious relationship between China and the USA in the South China Sea. China would not want military involvement in both areas at the same time. China has made claim to becoming an international power broker, principally through its Belt and Roads projects which already link it by treaty to many countries but creates a source of antagonism between it and western powers in general.

The G7 group of western nations is now proposing an economic forum which promises to fund infrastructure projects similar to those offered through China's Belt and Roads projects. China and the G7 countries should align their plans to their mutual benefit and also to the benefit of recipient countries. There does seem to be room for alignment of interests within the spheres of influence already proposed.

The issues of antagonism which this paper raises are of such significance that major conflicts between the three superpowers could arise, leading to conflict which would ultimately benefit nobody. It is suggested that should events arise, as this narrative forecasts, then a very significant opportunity will be presented to resolve problems which already exist, to the benefit of the major powers concerned and to humanity generally. The possibility of creating a prolonged period of peace and well-being should not be squandered. The principal superpowers must talk to each other with this goal in mind.

From The State Department of The USA: A Press Briefing

From our USA Defence Correspondent

Russia's eastern Siberia is only eighty-five miles of ocean from Alaska. We are naturally therefore always aware of what happens in our area of mutual interest. The USA always maintains a strong military, naval and air force presence in this area. Force levels have recently been increased as a consequence of Russia's belligerence towards its neighbours, including, in our case, recent extensive Russian navy and air force exercises in the Bering Sea. These exercises did not impinge on USA territory but were unusually extensive in scope and duration and were clearly intended to remind the USA of Russia's capability, acting as a form of warning to keep our distance. Russia's invasion of Ukraine has led to a heightened level of tension and awareness: Our reconnaissance activities have detected a reduction in army and air force levels in East Siberia. It is assumed that these reductions have been forced on Russia by the need to reinforce its military offensive in Ukraine. The recent published papers by China Forward raise serious issues in postulating very significant strategic changes in the ownership of territory in East Siberia. A position recommended by a think tank is no more than speculation, but it is known that this organisation has strong links with the Chinese Government and the suggestions made therefore have a level of credibility above that of pure speculation. Any changes in territorial ownership in eastern Siberia would dramatically change our relationship with both China and Russia. The USA would defend its own territorial position in Alaska and would take strong protective measures. Given the potential seriousness of any conflict, the USA therefore wishes to outline its own views on what China Forward is suggesting.

The position and requirements of the USA were stated at the Heads of Government meeting, which is detailed later in this narrative.

CHAPTER SIXTEEN

The Belarus Government Collapses

Russia moves in troops, further weakening its capability in Ukraine. EU heads of government agree and propose new borders in Russia, Sibir, China and the USA. Russia has problems maintaining its position in Ukraine and pulls out its army.

Belarus Government Collapses

Post-Conflict: Strategic Geopolitical Considerations

Russia in Ukraine

Withdrawal of Russian Forces from Ukraine

Belarus Government Collapses

From our Correspondent in Minsk

Belarus TV is entirely state controlled. It was therefore taken as fact when an announcement was made that the President of Belarus had been arrested and that the Chief of the General Staff had taken over the government. The reaction in Minsk was immediate. Crowds quickly gathered in the streets and there was public celebration. Traffic was halted, national flags were displayed and a party atmosphere prevailed. Further announcements on TV stated that the President of Belarus would be charged. The entire population was aware that the entire government was corrupt. The army chief of staff now appeared on TV. He announced that the army would hold power for as short a period as possible until fresh elections could be held. The departure of the President of Belarus was sufficient to justify celebration for the moment. Dealing with other corrupt luminaries could wait. This scenario was a pantomime. With Ukraine now protected by peacekeeping forces and Russia no longer hegemonic, the Belarus military chiefs now planned to disconnect from their past behaviour and hope for forgiveness.

Belarus had been an active partner with Russia in the invasion of Ukraine. Russian troops had been positioned in Belarus from where they attacked towards Kyiv. Belarus had originally planned on joining the assault but very wisely held back when Russia's clumsy drive to Kyiv quickly and obviously ran into trouble. Belarus played no other part in the invasion of Ukraine, despite threats to do so in later stages of the war. Taking note of the military and economic pressure piling up against Russia, the Belarus Army considered it wise to distance itself from its former master. Russia's reaction was rapid. Russian infantry appeared on the streets of Minsk within twelve hours. The TV station was taken over by Russian military authorities and celebrating crowds were told to clear the streets immediately. A curfew was declared with immediate effect, and this was enforced very quickly by Russian soldiers, who displayed no qualms about shooting anyone disobeying the curfew. Belarus was freed and un-freed in the space of twelve hours. The small Belarus army was unwilling and unable to even try to countermand their Russian masters. The Russian President was not prepared to have a slice of his empire taken away from him.

This turn of events had been anticipated by NATO, which had reinforced its positions in the neighbouring Baltic states but had no reason to intervene, given that Russia was already over-committed in the Donbas and southern Ukraine. NATO had planned on increasing the NATO holding force in the Baltic republics, and reinforcements were quickly flown in to man pre-positioned equipment. Elements of a NATO peacekeeping force were also moved to the Ukraine border in southern Belarus. Russia was now occupying five populated areas in neighbouring states in which it was not welcome: Abkhazia and Ossetia in Georgia, Belarus, Donbas, Crimea and southern Ukraine. It was spreading itself thinly, given the reduced force levels remaining to it, having already suffered such high casualty rates in Ukraine.

The removal of Belarus as a potential antagonist and the consequent additional burden on the Russian military relieved a little of the pressure on Ukraine and this was welcome. The additional burden on Russia's offensive capability was noted as increasing the potential for a successful offensive in the Donbas, by Ukrainian forces.

Post-conflict: Stategic Geopolitical Considerations

A Meeting of EU/NATO Heads of Government

Reported on by our Foreign Affairs Editor

Heads of government discussed the likely post-conflict situations in three areas:

1. The reduced circumstances of European Russia
2. The establishment of the new state of Sibir
3. The extent of the new territory added to the Chinese state in north-east Siberia

European Russia

The loss of almost the whole of Siberia and its annexed lands in the west will leave Russia much reduced geographically. Its population will also have been reduced by about twenty million now living in Sibir, but still leaving one of one hundred and ten million. Thus, it will remain the largest nation in Europe still controlled by an authoritarian military government and with a population very affected by propaganda which has consistently portrayed the west, including the USA within NATO, as enemies. The Russian people, whilst historically abused by successive regimes, from czardom through communism to autarky, remain a very proud and patriotic nation. They have been introduced to democracy, if grossly contaminated, in recent times and, it is anticipated, will look kindly on a regime democratically installed and supported by uncorrupt institutions based on the rule of law. We are going to the help of a nation under great stress, but we must remember its size and ambitions. We must carefully ensure that militarism does not raise its head again. Our first action must be to reduce the size of the military establishment, democratise its military governance and arrange for elections within six months, having freed all political prisoners. Security services, including the FSB, must be dismantled and regular police forces reinforced. The legal system is adequate if enforced in the interests of the people. In the background to the task of democratising state institutions lies the wish of the new Russian Government to join the EU. To create a situation in which the justice system, trade arrangements, free movement of people and many other complex factors can be reconciled to the existing

EU treaty will take many years. However, it does provide the opportunity for a significant leavening of the Russian bureaucracy, with existing EU civil servants to aid the transformation.

As heads of government, we are currently very concerned about the continuing existence of the Russian nuclear stockpile. We will insist, as part of the concurrent discussions concerning Russia's request to join NATO, that this concern is addressed, principally by effecting a very large reduction in its size. We are also particularly concerned to ensure that significant reductions in Russia's military capability are quickly implemented, alongside the assurance that protection of the Russian homeland will be provided by the continuing presence of NATO forces in the long term.

New Chinese Territory

In north-east Siberia, there is a scattering of villages occupied by small ethnic tribes, forced to settle there by Stalin in the 1930s. The USA state of Alaska lies to the north-east, separated from Siberia by the eighty-five kilometres-wide Bering Strait. The large island of Kamchatka, historically occupied by Japan, lies to the south-east. To the north is the East Siberian Sea, which becomes the Arctic Ocean. To the south are ranges of mountains stretching down to the Stanovoy Mountains, historically part of China.

The USA has declared that it would not be acceptable for a potentially hostile power to control north-east Siberia, including the Bering Strait. It therefore requires that Russia formally cedes the whole of the Kamchatka Peninsular and the area of Siberia north of the line of latitude of 150° to the USA. All military installations – army, air force and naval – will be surrendered also. With Russia's agreement, the original area ceded by China in 1858/60 and land to the east of Lake Baikal, historically Chinese, reverts to Chinese control. Land north of the Stanovoy Mountains should, in our view, now be identified as an adjunct to the Aigun Treaty lands and should also be ceded to China. It is suggested that the northern border lies one hundred kilometres south of Yakutsk, which is the principal city of the Republic of Sakha. The border should then lie directly to the east, meeting the Okhotsk Sea at Ekmen Point.

It will need to be agreed that standard maritime rules for inshore (twelve kilometres) and mineral rights (two hundred kilometres) in the East Siberia Sea and the Okhotsk and Bering seas are preserved, and that these seas are to be free for international shipping to use in accordance with international laws.

SIBIR

Siberia is huge, a total of about thirteen million square kilometres. It took Russia more than two hundred years to move east, destroying many of the ethnic peoples it met on the way. There are now about forty-five ethnic groups in Siberia. The largest are:

Buryats	:	About 450,000
Yakuts	:	440,000
Tuvas	:	320,000

Ethnic groups range in size, with the smallest counted in the low thousands. About six hundred thousand speak a variation of Mongolic, and the majority speak various Turkic languages. The three principal groups listed above are already a significant portion of the Russian republics named after them. The historical principal organisation seeking independence for those peoples was Raipon: the Russian Association of Indigenous Peoples of the North. The group itself is now tainted by its close association with the Russian state. Another independent group, headquartered in Norway, claims to represent the majority of ethnic clans/tribes. It is called the Centre for the Support of Indigenous Peoples of the North (CSIPN). It is banned in Russia. The total anticipated population of the new state of Sibir is approximately twenty million, comprising 4.5 million of ethnic origins and the balance made up of Siberiaks. A suggested border for Sibir to the east commences on the River Lena at the new Chinese border, which is one hundred kilometres south of Yakutsk, due east, following the Chinese border to Enken Point on the Okhotsk Sea. It then follows the sea coast to meet the new USA border in north-east Sibir and follows that border to meet the Arctic Sea. To the west, the border matches that of the new Russian border, starting in the Kara Sea and following the line of latitude 70° until it meets the Kazakhstan border. It then follows the Kazakhstan and Mongolian borders until it moves north around the east borders of the Buryatia Republic to head north along the eastern shore of Lake Baikal, following the Chinese border north to the junctions of borders at the River Lena. The border proposed is shown on the map.

Sibir will be a very large country. Given the diversity of ethnic mix and the distances between components, it is assumed that a federal state structure will be required. The original ethnic populations will centre on

Sakha (Yakutia), Tuva and Buryatia. The largest Siberiak populations will be found in Krasnoyarsk (2.95 million), Novokusnetsk (500,000) and Ulan-Ude (400,000). The new state will have economic strength from the date of inauguration. The main complaint of the Siberian population has been that the large proportion of mineral wealth and locally raised taxes was consumed by Moscow and European Russia. The people of Sibir will now find a treasure chest of assets available. The converse of this situation is that Moscow, with its new depleted land mass and resources, will need to reorder its resources to survive.

Democratic principles are more strongly adhered to in Siberia than in Russia, but the fusing together of such a diverse ethnic mix will be achieved only after a long period of cohabitation. The initial blooming of a new nation such as this will require significant political, economic and internal support, which will need to be provided for by a mix including EU and southern neighbouring countries, the IMF and the World Bank. It is suggested that the UN resurrects the mandate system practised when Britain was mandated by the League of Nations in 1922 to administer and govern Palestine with a view to allowing it to achieve independence. It is suggested that the EU Commission could perform the same function in Sibir. The UN must certainly be involved. This nation-building exercise will require more international effort than can be summarised here.

The heads of government concluded their meeting, expressing a realisation that they had done no more than provide an initial start point from where further negotiations could proceed.

The final situation raised at the heads of EU countries meeting concluded that the three states bordering Sibir and involved in its creation, that is, Russia, China and the USA, will include within their border ethnic groups which would be better situated in Sibir. The UN Assembly vote which will be required to set up the new state must require of these three countries that they afford these ethnic groups the financial and physical means to allow them, including populations and assets, to peacefully migrate to within Sibir if they wish.

Russia in Ukraine

A position paper created by our Defence Editor

After months of fighting, the Russian invading army fought for and retained control of Crimea, most of the Donbas and Luhansk. It lost Kherson and failed to capture Odesa and was never able to control central Ukraine. The Ukrainian Army was reorganised and reinforced, with wide-ranging and up-to-date equipment provided by NATO. Fighter aircraft were purchased from neighbouring countries. Thus, the Kyiv government held country extending from the Polish frontier to Kharkiv on the Russian border, with significant depth north and south. No ceasefire between Russia and the Kyiv government was ever properly declared. The Ukrainian Army continued to encroach on Russian-held territory, and guerrilla attacks were a daily occurrence, with significant losses caused to Russian equipment and personnel. Attempts to limit this damage and to subdue and control the population in the areas they controlled required a large military presence supported by FSB and police drawn from Russia. The internationally recognised government in Kyiv retained its seat in the UN and was given preliminary entry status to the EU and to NATO. The EU and the IMF granted multi-billion Euro loans to allow a start on reconstruction of war damage in cities under its control. Kyiv also lodged with the UN a claim for five hundred billion dollars against Russia for rebuilding costs. In general, the area controlled by Kyiv was peaceful, with a reviving economy and a significant military capability to deter further aggression. The Russian-controlled area of Ukraine was under constant assault by guerrilla groups, with no funding available for reconstruction or to revitalise a moribund economy. It was now a major drain on Russian economic and military resources, and local civilian morale was very low amongst Russian speakers. In late 2022, Russia announced a partial mobilisation of three hundred thousand recruits to strengthen its position in Ukraine. It is anticipated that it will have problems in training and equipping the new units expected to be formed. This move should influence the war to their advantage, but it is likely that it will take longer and be less effective than Russia expects. In the meantime, the prolongation of the war has brought about civil disobedience and street protests to many Russian cities.

Withdrawal of Russian Forces from Ukraine

A press release from NATO HQ

Russia's position in Siberia, given the success of the Chinese advance, has become desperate. Russia now appears to be regrouping almost all the units engaged with the Ukrainian Army and redeploying them inside the Russian border. It has also reduced garrisons in Transnistria and Kaliningrad to small holding forces which would be unable to resist any organised military pitted against them but are hopefully capable of controlling the local population. It appears to have decided that holding its position in Ukraine requires more effort than it is prepared to deploy and is withdrawing its army units from all but the Donbas and Crimea areas, reverting to the areas gained in 2014, leaving very limited military presence and relying on local militia to hold their ground.

Freed of almost all military opposition, the Kyiv army went on the offensive, immediately confronting the local militia in the Donbas. Within two weeks, the Russian- backed militia in the Donbas and Crimea collapsed. They were no match for the reorganised and reinforced Ukrainian Army. The army moved up to the Russian border and Kyiv was able to announce that Ukraine including Crimea had been freed of its invaders.

CHAPTER SEVENTEEN

A Second Meeting of Russian and EU/NATO Delegates hear of NATO's plans to confront the Chinese invaders

Second Meeting of Russian/NATO Delegates

A Day in the Life of Andrei Garasimov

A Story told by Matvey Lavrov

Second meeting of Russian/NATO Delegates to discuss NATO help to Russia

Opening remarks by the Secretary General of NATO

From our Defence Correspondent

1. The foreign ministers of the EU, with NATO participation, have met and discussed the military positions of both Russia and China, have agreed in principle that the EU, and in particular that NATO, will deploy sufficient force, when combined with the remaining Russian army, to resist encroachment of Chinese forces beyond a boundary which military and political logic will decide.
    i. The Russian Government agreed the outcome of the meeting of heads of government of EU Member States and the obligations it placed on it.
    ii. The Russian Government led by its President had rejected the proposals put forward by the EU, but this position changed rapidly when the President, his Defence Minister and the Chief of the General Staff were removed from power. The replacement government acceded to the terms offered.

2. The military position is as follows:
    a. Chinese forces have advanced and hold a line between Belogorsk and Blagoveshchensk, where they appear to have halted to consolidate and reorganise what has become a long logistic chain. However, they have military units inside China operating along the main road G202 and able to interfere with Russian forces retreating on the west on the north side of the Amur River. The river does limit their effect. It is anticipated that no further major movement will occur for approximately two weeks. The force opposing the Russians at their next encounter are likely to be at least two hundred thousand personnel, with up to one thousand tanks plus other armoured vehicles. The Chinese already have and will maintain air superiority.
    b. Russian forces are retreating somewhat in disarray – NATO HQ has been in touch with military headquarters in the Kremlin. NATO forces sufficient to make an impact on the military situation confronting the Russian Army are already in a state of high alert, but it will take two to three weeks for a substantial force to be deployed east of the Urals. The tactical plan made jointly by NATO and the Kremlin is for the Russian East Army to take up a defensive position centred around Mogacha and along the Amazar, Shilka and Tungir Rivers and the marshy ground around the rivers. The force will be reinforced by Russian army units freed from Ukraine and able to deploy fairly quickly along the Siberian Railway and the M58 road east of Moscow. The Russian Army should be able to hold up the advancing Chinese force for long enough to allow a NATO force to be deployed further to the west. The force was also to be reinforced by 5th Guards Tank Division based in Buratya and elements of the Air Defence Army based in Chito. Remaining elements of 41st and 35th Combined Arms Combat Armies retreating from Khabarovsk will also participate.
    c. The battle plan for the main NATO force will be for it to secure the area south of Lake Baikal to the Mongolian frontier. This plan will tie in with the EU's proposal to accept Lake Baikal as the westernmost line which the Chinese will be allowed to reach. This line will also be the proposed easternmost boundary of a new federal nation of Sibir.

d. NATO forces will not be deployed to the east of Lake Baikal. Diplomatic discussions are already being held between the EU (with Russia) and the Chinese Government with the aim of minimising the possibility of confrontation between NATO and Chinese forces at Lake Baikal. As a consequence of these discussions, a ceasefire between Russia (and NATO forces) and China should lead to total cessation of hostilities between the two countries and acceptance of the new international boundaries.

A day in the life of Andrei Garasimov

Sergeant: 242 Tank Regiment, Sibirtevo, Siberia
Dictated to our Correspondent in Khabarovsk Military Hospital

We were told that the Chinese had invaded Russia and were advancing on Khabarovsk. We were directly north of one of their advancing columns. We were told that the column was tank heavy, with supporting infantry in armoured personnel carriers. My tank crew consisted of myself as tank commander, Grego Karasimov, driver, and Oleg Kasporov, gun loader. We normally crewed a T64 tank but most of our tanks, T64s and T72s, had been withdrawn for deployment in Ukraine. We were personally fond of our original tank, which had been maintained in good order; its 125mm smooth bore gun polished and greased with its brass aiming sight polished and gleaming like a mirror. The 7.62 mm machine gun fitted coaxially with the main gun and the turret mounted anti-aircraft 12.7mm cannon were treated in the same way. Unfortunately, our tank had been sent to Ukraine and our main task now was to refurbish a replacement T64, taken out of store. Our base held almost two hundred of these stored tanks. I am told that between 1962 and 1987, about one hundred thousand of these machines were manufactured. The stock in our care has not been properly maintained. The tank we were to work on had to be towed to our unit workshop, where about thirty others were undergoing the same process. None of them were fit for operational duty. In our case, the internal bore of the main gun was so rusty that the cleaning rod could not be passed through.

The breach was rusted and a sledgehammer had to be used to free it. The aiming site was missing, as was the heavy machine gun. Both items had been removed as a routine cannibalisation activity to be fitted to other tanks further forward in their own restoration routines. We were able to obtain replacement items to achieve operational ability. We dare not start the diesel engine as it had been unused for so long that it was assumed to have rusty bores. To attempt starting it without pre-maintenance would have, at a minimum, caused bore damage, and total blow-up a possibility. The engine had to be removed, stripped to its component parts and rebuilt. The process also applied to starter motor, gear box and clutches. There were other problems too numerous to mention.

We had been working on the tank for about two months when the invasion alarm was sounded. Within two days, we were able to declare the tank operational, i.e., it started, travelled on its tracks and had a traversable main gun. The next problem within the unit was to get the tank south to meet our fellow regimented tanks, which had already moved south. Unfortunately, the majority of our tank transporters had gone to Ukraine with our original tanks and were either somewhere else in Siberia or still in Ukraine. We were forced to move on our own tracks. The holding area for our regiment was about forty-five kilometres south of Khabarovsk. We set off in columns. We now numbered about seventy-five tanks. Four were T72s – original stock – and the balance almost entirely refurbished T64s. Within five kilometres, at least eight T64s had broken down and had to wait for recovery. Just as with our tank transporters, most recovery vehicles had been shipped out with our original T64 and T72 tank stock, so recovery takes a long time. On arrival at our holding areas, still with a functioning tank, our unit was down to a total of forty-five operational vehicles. The activity associated with the preparation of our tank and the move had rather lessened the concern we felt at the prospect of action. This came on the morrow, when thirty of our tanks, accompanied by about forty infantry armoured personnel carriers, were ordered to mount an attack on a frontage of two kilometres towards woodland, about three kilometres to our front. Our Chinese antagonists were presumably sheltering and covered by the woodland. The first kilometre was uneventful. Then all hell broke loose. Our unit was shelled by 152mm calibre artillery; randomly in the area of our attacking formation but causing mayhem, with shell bursts rattling the tank armour and, inevitably, achieving direct hits on at least five tanks, which immediately burst into flames. The initial conflagration caused by an artillery round striking a tank would be followed by an even larger explosion when the thirty or so main gun rounds stored in the turret exploded, invariably blowing off the tank turret, which flew at least five metres into the air, followed by the crew. It was a spectacular sight, but we were very aware that each tank crew of three would have been invariably burnt to a crisp and then torn apart by the force of the detonation of their own ammunition.

Driving onwards was a sick-making sensation, contemplating our own end. That end came in the form of armed drones. At least fifteen of them circled over the attacking tanks. Many of them dropped anti-armour bombs, one of which was accurately directed at our tank. The weapon exploded on the rear of the tank on the engine casing. A shortage of explosive deflector plates in the unit meant that none were placed on the engine bay cover. The bomb went straight through to the engine. The tank reverberated with the explosive shock, but the armour plate between the turret and the engine compartment provided a short protective delay which allowed all three crew members to fling open the top hatches and abandon the vehicle. We were now only about five hundred metres from the enemy positions and small arms fire was immediately aimed at us. It was concentrated fire which struck down Gregory, who died instantly with a large hole in his back. Oleg lasted about ten seconds before a small cannon round took away most of his head, a lot of which ended up all over my overalls. I suppose I would call myself lucky because a small arms round smashed into my lower leg and prevented me from trying my luck by moving on. I lay where I fell, lost consciousness and awoke in darkness. It took me two hours to drag myself and my damaged leg to our original attack start point. Luck came my way again, as there were still soldiers around who were able to carry me off to a first aid station and so to hospital.

I was briefed later that the attack was a total disaster. Most attacking tanks were destroyed, and those which were not were abandoned by the crews, many of whom were then shot as they tried to escape. Given the quality of modern Chinese tanks, I do not suppose that our abandoned T64s would be much use to them. In Stalin's day, an attack like ours would have been preceded by a fierce artillery barrage, followed by waves of attacking infantry and tanks, our case, we had no artillery, which like our tanks, had been despatched to Ukraine, and there were no follow-up echelons to support the initial attacking wave. Most of the remaining tanks of the regiment would be those which had broken down and were possibly recoverable. At least my war was over, with part of my leg gone and no question of my repeating my short-lived effort to do my duty.

This account was dictated by Matvey Lavrov to our correspondent during a visit to a field hospital in Irkutsk

My name is Matvey Lavrov. I am a private soldier in 1st Company, 4th Premier Battalion, 5th Infantry Brigade of the Russian Army. My barrack is in Khabarovsk but I have been working in various locations near Birobidzhan. We were told that Chinese armoured units had advanced to within twenty-five kilometres of our position. Our assigned task was in support of an armoured artillery regiment. On that day, we were tasked with unloading 152mm rounds from a railcar into wheeled cargo lorries and also directly into tracked guns where they could move alongside the railcars. The rounds were stacked loose in the railcars. Each round, which weighed over 35 kilogrammes, had to be manually lifted and carried onto the parked lorry or passed directly to the gun crew alongside the railcar. It was very exhausting work, with rest stops every thirty minutes. On past occasions, when doing this work, rounds had arrived crated, and if a forklift was available, which was not very often, the machine did most of the lifting and cross loading was much more quickly achieved. No forklift was available today, so the work rate became slower and slower. We had almost reached the limits of our physical capability when work was stopped in a most dramatic way by the scream of arriving shells which suddenly started to burst around our work area. The shelling was so accurate that it must have been directed either by GPS guidance or by a surveillance drone flying overhead. In theory, our local air defence cover should have given us some warning. Unfortunately, our air defence cover had been so depleted in our hasty retreat to the west that its absence came as no surprise. Even if we had spotted a drone, we were only equipped with small arms to defend ourselves and would probably not have succeeded in shooting it down. The shelling was sudden and relentless. An area one kilometre wide and half a kilometre deep, an area the artillery called a 'stonk' and straddling the ammunition train we were unloading, was struck by shells arriving at a rate of four or five per minute.

Each screaming shell gave almost no notice of its arrival. On arrival at the site, we had automatically provided ourselves with protective shell scrapes no more than fifty centimetres deep, to provide at least some cover in the event of an enemy attack. I was close to one scrape and leapt straight into it. It provided minimum cover. Any shell landing within two metres or so of it would have mixed my remains with earth and made me part of the crater. I hoped that no shell had my name on it. Fortunately, it did not, but quite a few had 'ammunition train' written on them, again, fortunately not close to my section of train, but there was an enormous explosion about fifty metres from me. A crimson flash seared upwards about fifty metres into the air, accompanied by the wreckage of rolling stock and a roaring blast wave which filled my shell scrape with sand, stones, bits of metal and a boot with a foot in it.

Shelling stopped after just five minutes. Our enemy in the air had signalled a success message to the distant guns, whose operatives must have been well pleased at the catastrophic damage they had caused: half the ammunition train had been destroyed, ten lorries had been reduced to smoking and twisted chassis remains, and six tanks had been reduced to scrap iron; all of them had suffered internal explosions which flung the turrets into the air and reduced the crews to ashes. A head count of our company later revealed that twenty were totally unaccounted for, presumably blown to pieces, a further forty were counted but dead and forty-five were injured, some very badly. Our company had been reduced from one hundred and fifty to forty-five, all in a state of shock. Our company had essentially ceased to exist as a working unit, the remaining soldiers being sent to the rear.

Assumptions that the much-reduced combat strength of the Russian East Army will be able to delay the Chinese Invasion Force East of Lake Baikal

A major NATO armoured force of 200,000 will be positioned west of Ulan-Ude. A force commanded by France will protect the area north of Lake Baikal. The USA, with Canada, will secure the oil and gas fields of Western Siberia.

> *Russia Cannot Repulse the Chinese Incursion into the Amur Valley*
>
> *A Report from NATO Headquarters confirming NATO involvement*
>
> *Defensive NATO Build-up, South of Lake Baikal*
>
> *West Siberia Oil and Gas Fields*
>
> *NATO, USA and Canada in the West Siberia Fields*

Russia cannot repulse The Chinese incursion into The Amur Valley

Data taken from a statement released by the UK Minister of Defence
From our Defence Correspondent

Russia has an economy no bigger than that of Canada, a twelfth smaller than that of the USA and one tenth that of China. Russian defence expenditure has traditionally been maintained at a high level, consuming a large part (20% plus?) of its GDP in order to maintain a much larger military force than was rational, given the size of its GDP. It did this by holding down the quality of living for most of its population, but the commitment to this level of expenditure on an overstretched economy did not provide for the expenditure required to create and maintain a military force adequate for modern warfare. This situation was reflected in the overall performance of the field army committed to the invasion of Ukraine.

Following the Battle of the Amur, the field army could be divided into three segments:

1. Russia had deployed 50% of its combat capability against Ukraine. It failed to meet its objectives against a smaller and more lightly armed Ukrainian army. Russia deployed the best half of its army, equipped with the most up-to-date equipment available to it. However, it became evident that budget limitations had affected the numbers of the most modern armour available. This was evidenced by the widespread deployment of T62/64/72 tanks: obsolete by western standards. There was a demonstrable shortage of logistic vehicles, inadequate air defence weapons, and the Russian air force was unable to gain even partial air superiority. There appeared to be inadequate numbers of infantry available to support armour, which was constantly being ambushed, and morale was not good. Nevertheless, the force which had invaded Ukraine was of reasonable quality, and despite the fact that it lost at least 25% of its personnel and armour in action against the Ukrainian Army, and despite the constant losses caused by Ukrainian guerrilla warfare, the remaining force of about two hundred thousand personnel and fifteen hundred pieces of armour was capable of becoming an effective force able to confront the Chinese incursion if deployed in time.

2. The Eastern Siberian Army had been stripped of its most effective units and equipment to reinforce the army in the west: both for the original invasion of Ukraine and unforeseen requirement to be prepared to confront a NATO alliance significantly reinforced on its western borders. The East Army could not be adequately rebuilt and was therefore in no condition to withstand the Chinese invasion. Its calamitous retreat from Vladivostok and Khabarovsk hardly improved its condition. The consequent Battle of the Amur Valley sealed its fate, and its retreat towards Lake Baikal was more of a rout than a withdrawal. It could not be expected to play a significant part in succeeding hostilities.

3. In theory, Russia possessed a very large reserve force of up to a million personnel. But little could be expected of this reserve of ill-equipped manpower. Personnel were very poorly trained, had little if any equipment beyond personal weapons and no effective armour. Its main use as a reserve was in the provision of poorly trained personnel to infill units which had suffered heavy battlefield casualties in Ukraine.

Summary

By the time of the Chinese incursion, a theoretical Russian standing army of at least six hundred thousand combat personnel had been reduced by more than 50%, with matching armour and artillery. The Russian air force had suffered a similar reduction in capability. The Russian state had not for many years had the financial and industrial ability to sustain armed forces which in any way matched the capability of which it boasted. Its adventure in Ukraine had cost it grievously in military and economic terms, and it was left unprepared to face a Chinese attack with significantly larger and better equipped army and air force. Except for its nuclear arsenal, its days as a significant military superpower were clearly over and its state strategy now had to be how to extricate itself from the disastrous situation in which it now found itself.

Reporting from NATO Headquarters: NATO involved in Siberia

From our Correspondents with NATO HQ and with NATO assembling in Siberia

We received the extraordinary news that Russia has sought assistance from NATO in halting Chinese forces advancing from eastern Siberia. Also, that NATO has agreed to provide assistance. The current situation regarding the disposition of Russian and Chinese forces was described in yesterday's edition. Consequent on the war in Ukraine, all NATO countries had, for some months, been activating their military forces. They were thus ready to assemble significant military assets very quickly. This dispatch was provided by our reporter located at the railway station in Ulan-Ude, which will become the forward defensive position adopted by NATO forces. The town has a population of about four hundred thousand: sixty percent Sibiraks with the remainder comprising various ethnicities, mainly

Buryats. The town has been selected as a forward focus for NATO activity as it sits on the east/west Trans-Siberian Railway from Moscow to Vladivostok and is also the terminal of the Manchurian Railway which ran across the Gobi Desert to Beijing about twelve hundred kilometres away. The main west/east Siberian trunk road also passes through the town. The existing Chinese border is about two hundred kilometres away, south of Lake Baikal, which presents a significant obstacle to east/west movement, and about one hundred kilometres to the west of Ulan-Ude. The town therefore presented a choke point to any movement from east to west at this point, and also an obstacle to military movement north from China into southern Siberia through Mongolia. To the Russian forces confronting the Chinese Army in East Siberia, NATO's deployment represented a fall-back position, providing military and physiological assurance to stiffen their resolve, given the very heavy pressure being applied by a rapidly advancing Chinese army. The NATO forces deployed in and around Ulan-Ude, but mainly to its west, are focused on the 7th Division deployed from the UK. In recent years, the British Army has been significantly reduced in strength and until recently had only one unit of brigade strength available for rapid deployment. Given the dangerously evolving conflict in eastern Siberia, the army hastily formed a second brigade. Both reinforced brigades now consisted of three armoured vehicle mounted infantry battalions, each of about eight hundred soldiers, and two regiments with about sixty Chieftain tanks. Divisional supporting units consisted of two regiments of tracked armour artillery units providing a total of about thirty-six 155mm guns, a regiment of Royal Engineers, a reconnaissance squadron of scimitar armoured vehicles, backup of repair workshops, a squadron of six Apache attack helicopters, a field hospital and logistic support units. The British contingent amounts to a division of about twelve thousand soldiers: by itself insufficient to deter a Chinese force of the size likely to be encountered across a front of up to two hundred kilometres, linking Lake Baikal to the Kamar, Mali and Zaganskiy mountain ranges. The British forces have been reinforced by a division from Ukraine, in the process of being formally welcomed into NATO, and equivalent forces from Romania, Italy, Poland, Germany and Finland, other nations provided a total of about one hundred and fifty aircraft based at Irkutsk airfield and commanded also by an officer from the British Royal Air Force.

The notes assembled above were prepared at a NATO conference hosted at the NATO force headquarters in Irkutsk.

Defensive NATO build-up south of Lake Baikal

A second report from our Defence Correspondent embedded with the NATO force in Irkutsk

The UK Standby Brigade had been the first NATO force to reach the designated defensive area to the south of Lake Baikal. It was rapidly followed by the NATO Standby Brigade. Subsequent arrivals by brigade-strength units from the Baltic countries, the equivalent of a division each from Ukraine, Romania and Italy, and major units from other NATO countries, very quickly reached a force level of two hundred thousand personnel in the area. Up to a thousand tanks were being quickly mobilised throughout Europe, some arriving by road and the bulk via the Siberian Railway. Very early planning by NATO Headquarters, anticipating problems arising which would inevitably affect Europe, had paid off handsomely. NATO air forces quickly assembled on airfields in the eastern NATO countries and on Ukrainian airfields. Aircraft were also positioned within range of the potential conflict area. The original plan to feed the remains of the Russian Army in the west, to assist the East Army confronting the Chinese, was abandoned as creating a logistical problem getting them through Ulan-Ude, given the additional complexity of very significant numbers of NATO troops and equipment moving through West Russia. The tactical decision taken by NATO and Russian General Staff was to instruct the Russian Army in the east to create strongpoints to hold Chinese forces for as long as possible and to narrow the defensive front defended in order to concentrate forces. What remained of the Russian air force was to apply maximum support in a ground attack role in support of local operation of the East Army. The Russian Army in the west was now given a reserve blocking position behind the assembled NATO force.

Following NATO HQ instructions, only any necessary defensive combat activities were carried out against Chinese military units at this stage. Assembling this very large NATO force was a major logistical achievement. Fortunately, forward-looking plans and significant pre-positioning of equipment, munitions, repair, support and medical facilities had already taken place. Although a very major logistic effort continued, the NATO force was in good order and able to confront any Chinese incursion. Chinese forces were now at the end of an extended logistic support system, potentially subject to interdiction. NATO forces now waited for events to unfold.

A footnote by our defence correspondent

The commander of the force has no doubt that his combined force, now renamed One Corps, will be capable of stopping the significant Chinese force which is being monitored as it moves forward. His force will hold the Chinese force moving east to west and also any Chinese movement approaching from the south along the line of the Trans-Mongolian Railway, which, in any case, would be confronted by the Mongolian Army. Mountain ranges impede movement from the east and south, and attacking armoured forces will present good targets for NATO aircraft operating from Irkutsk. He is confident that his force will hold the area around Lake Baikal and stop the Chinese at that point. The area south of Lake Baikal is seen as a potential defensible border between China and any new state created to its west. It is the view of the EU that the western border of any newly acquired Chinese land should be at the eastern shore of Lake Baikal.

NATO recognises the desire of the Chinese to occupy the Baikal region, and especially north of the lake where oil and gas wells are located which supply both through pipelines to China. Movement to the north of the lake is difficult, and the lake is about six hundred kilometres long. At the north of the lake, a French division, with Norwegian support, is to be based around Severobaykalsk to block any east-west movement along the only road in that region.

West Siberia oil/gas fields. NATO protection required

A paper by our Defence Editor

West Siberian oil and gas fields are vast in extent, stretching south from the Kara Sea to north of Yekaterinburg, Omsk and Novosibirsk. The fields constitute the bulk of Russian oil, gas and mineral reserves and are consequently a major part of the Russian economy. The Ural Mountains provide a natural eastern physical boundary to the Russian state, separating it from Siberia. In addition to oil, gas and other minerals, a significant proportion of Russian industry is also located east of the mountains. Thus, this area had to be provided with NATO protection.

Notes on a NATO briefing session below discuss this requirement

At the start of the Russian President's war in Ukraine, western Europe was a major customer for Russia's oil and gas. For example, Germany drew fifty-five percent of its gas for industrial and domestic use from Russian sources. As the war progressed and western countries increased their backing for Ukraine, the Russian President began to use the reduction of gas supplies to the west as a form of blackmail in an attempt to reduce western support for Ukraine. Eventually, gas supplies were cut off completely. Reliance on Russia was now regarded as a strategic error, and western Europe planned to move away from such reliance by finding alternative sources of energy. This process will continue unaffected by the outcome of the Ukrainian War. However, Russia will eventually be able to export elsewhere, with such exports eventually being central to its economic future. Russia's hydrocarbon reserves remain a European asset which must be protected.

NATO (US) protection: Information extracted from a NATO briefing

From our Defence Correspondent

The military resources of western European countries are deployed countering a Chinese military intrusion and protecting East Siberian oil/gas fields. They would have difficulty in also protecting the West Siberian oil/gas fields. It is anticipated that the Chinese would regard the Lake Baikal area and the surrounding oil/gas fields as a priority strategic target. The NATO commander at Baikal anticipates that his force will be able to hold the Lake Baikal area. A separate NATO force is required to operate in West Siberia.

North American (US and Canadian) ground and air forces will provide protection to the West Siberian fields. The original agreement reached with the Russian Government was that American forces would not be called upon without further agreement, given the great sensitivity of Russia to such a development. However, given the continuing inability of Russian forces to hold back the Chinese advance, the involvement of US/Canada has become necessary to ensure protection of the West Siberian fields. This will be done.

Deployment of American (Canadian) forces in West Siberia

This news item is based on a brief provided by NATO and a follow-up meeting with the commander of US (NATO) forces based at Talnakh

The area is far from current hostilities and is, in any case, far from areas of potential interest to China, being a great distance from their homeland. Nevertheless, the possibility of local actions to the rear of Russian defensive forces and of sabotage cannot be ruled out. All the oil/gas facilities are already provided with local security by the commercial companies which run them. The additional protection provided by NATO will take the form of local garrisons of armoured infantry, with personnel and heavy lift helicopter backup. NATO will deploy two divisions of three brigades each. Each brigade will cover an area of about one thousand square kilometres. Their function will be the provision of rapid infantry and light armour support if any problems arise. The division headquarters and Corps headquarters will be located at Nagorsk and Talnakh. The force allocated to the defence of the West Siberian fields will be commanded by the USA.

CHAPTER NINETEEN

Russia withdraws from East Siberia. Local hostilities end

The outcome of the Battle of the River Amur is that Russia's 35th and 41st Combined Arms Armies retire to the west. Remaining Russian forces withdrawn to barracks. Financial and logistic arrangements are made to sustain Russian assets now controlled by China.

Hostilities in East Siberia

End of Operations in East Siberia

A mine clearing operation by Corporal Jin Mau

The Story of a River Crossing: By Lieutenant Alexsandr Zhukov

Tanks used as Artillery: By Corporol Artemus Smirnov

Hostilities in East Siberia

From our Correspondent

Russia had not really expected China to invade Russian East Siberia despite the obvious signs of such an intention. Thus, although local commanders prepared themselves for an event, anticipated force movements, including logistic stockpiling and troop movements, did not take place.

The Russian 3rd Combat Army and the 270 Motor Rifle Division, both based in Khabarovsk, bore the brunt of the Chinese invasion heading east and north, whilst the 55th Marine Division defended Vladivostok, where it was based. Russian units in Sakhalin and Kamchatka were not involved. The inadequate and under-strength units were no match for the Chinese invaders and, leaving garrisons in Khabarovsk and Vladivostok, they were forced to retire to the west, after a week of combat, through Khabarovsk. The Chinese thrusts heading north across the River Amur met with serious resistance from 41st Combined Arms Army and 74th Motor Rifle Brigade, both based in Novosibirsk, and the 35th Combined Arms Army based in Belogorsk. Russian defensive actions along the length of the River Amur allowed the surviving elements of the forces fighting to the east to retire (retreat) to the west. This movement west was a disorderly route, with most units left in a condition which would prevent them from taking any further part in operations without reorganising and re-equipping: both unlikely events, given Russia's condition. However, some elements of the 35th and 41st Armies were expected to be part of the Mogacha defensive position on the Amazar River.

End of operations in East Siberia

The Russian 35th and 41st Armies had held back the Chinese offensive across the River Amur for long enough for some elements of Russian forces fighting east of Khabarovsk to retreat to the west. Both armies continued to fight rearguard actions to preserve what it could of their strength whilst also retiring to the west. However, the congestion caused by the very large movement of troops and armoured vehicles, all heading west at the same time, was very much beyond the capacity of the single motorway, the M60, to contain. The same road also had to provide for logistic support traffic moving east in support of the 35th and 41st Armies. Thus, an order was issued limiting western movements to elements of the 35th and 41st Armies only. All other units were ordered to cease operation and return to barracks. In effect, this was capitulation by the Russian East Army, and this was notified to the Chinese Army involved and a ceasefire was agreed. All Russian equipment was to be left in situ. Personnel were to return to barracks.

In discussions between Russia and Chinese military commanders, arranged through their governments, it was also agreed that units of the 35th and 41st Armies would be allowed to retire westwards as far as Lake Baikal to join NATO forces assembling there, without interference. There was an anticipation of a ceasefire and cessation of hostilities. Agreement was reached by both governments that Russia would continue to supply, in a short term to be agreed, the necessary financial and logistic support to allow military units and civilian populations in areas under Chinese control to survive. Hostilities in the east of eastern Siberia had thus been brought to a close. Action to be taken to the west of that area was on the point of being discussed in meetings between the EU/NATO and the Chinese Government.

Anti-Tank Minefield Clearing: Recollections by Corporal Jin Man

This is an extract from an article published in the Beijing edition of the Peoples Daily. The article sets out to glorify the achievements of Chinese soldiers who have been awarded medals for bravery in action.

Corporal Jin Man serves in the 21st Engineer Company of the 25th Armoured Division of The Peoples Liberation Army of China, normally based in Harbin but now part of the force attacking Khabarovsk. He tells his story :-

I had been attached to a tank squadron which had come across a minefield laid by the russians across the main road from the south into the city. A one hundred metre section of the road had been destroyed by repeated passes of what we call 'dragons tooth' ploughs. These were massive single blade ploughs towed behind a tank or bulldozer which rip up the road to a depth of eighty centimetres and leave behind mounds of broken road material. A few passes of these ploughs made movement along the road impossible for all but tracked vehicles. The russians had then mined the debris. Our tanks could have travelled over the rubble but the anti-tank mines made this hazardous. Two of our tanks tried to push on but both were immobilised. The first activated a tilt fuse which detonated under its belly; the least protected tank hull area. The crew members were killed by the detonation. The second was halted when it activated a shallower buried mine which cut its tracks. The crew dismounted but were killed by machine gun fire. The ground either side of the road was marshland which would bog down any tank trying to cross it. If our tank attack was to succeed the mines sown in the rubble had to be cleared. It fell to the sappers of my company to undertake this task. A reconnaissance party was sent out to examine the target area on the first night.

The mines found by the reconnaissance party were the TM6 anti-tank mine containing 9kg of explosive armed by a screw-in fuse. They also found the M14 anti-personnel mine armed by removing a split pin. The TM6 was capable of destroying the track and running gear of a tank whilst the M14 would blow off at least a soldier's foot. These mines were routinely sown around anti-tank mines. The reconnaissance party found more tilt-activated fuses and anti-tank mines laid in pairs, two feet deep, one on top of the other, to trick any unwary searcher. In some cases, anti-tank mines had been laid on top of armed anti-personnel mines, causing detonation of both if the top mine was moved. The combination of these simple but very effective traps presented us with a very complex and hazardous clearing operation. Clearing the mines by day, in virtual sight of the enemy, was impossible and clearing by night was dangerous on the assumption that the enemy had night vision equipment. I was not involved in the mine clearance operation mounted on the first night but I was aware that the company had lost forty men killed or wounded by enemy fire, having cleared only twenty metres of road. My section was ordered to continue the operation on the second night. I felt sick at the prospect of what lay ahead. If a mine blows up under you, your remains would fit into a plastic shopping bag. There would be no body bag and no last rites. Death was instant and you had no time to think about whatever joy or sadness would otherwise have come your way. But what was worse was the mine clearing process itself: waiting for a detonation. Although you would not be aware of instantaneous oblivion, the constant gut-wrenching fear preyed on you for every second when carrying out a process which might cause an explosion. This was a huge physiological burden impossible to brush aside. I was very very frightened of what lay ahead.

Given time to prepare, at least some actions were in hand to reduce casualties. I hoped that this sentiment played a part in my superiors' calculations. What they probably regarded as much more important was the need to clear the road quickly at whatever cost. These actions included intermittent and counter battery artillery fire on the enemy lines ahead, almost constant small arms fire aimed at potential enemy infantry positions and a smoke screen to partially hide our activities.

Night came and we set off. We could tell where our start point was by the sight of the residual remains of what had previously been our friends, laying across our path. We operated in teams of five men. Each team searched a road area about three paces wide. Five teams were required to cover the road width. We would normally stagger the start times to minimise the effect of an explosion but, as expected, the need for speed took precedence over caution and all five teams started clearing at the same time. In the lead was our detector man who swept the width of our pathway with his magnetic sweeper. Mines contain very small amounts of detectable metal and electronic sweeping has to be very carefully carried out. The detector man was followed by a man who rechecked the ground by prodding with a pole or bayonet to feel for any mine missed by the initial sweep and to defuse, lift and mark any mine found by either. Marked mines would be moved to the roadside or detonated in situ.

Number three in the team had the task of picking up the disarmed mines and carrying them to the roadside to be destroyed by controlled detonation later. Numbers four and five team members helped with mine removal and also marked with pegged tape the mine free lane which had been created. All these team tasks were stressful but rotation between men took place to at least reduce the immediate physiological pain. The battlefield scenario included our own artillery fire, small arms fire from our own side and desultory machine gun fire and artillery from the enemy. Our own smoke screen helped to hide us but made our immediate task more difficult to control. We pressed on.

The first upset occurred when a major mine explosion hit the team working to our left. Two of the team seemed to have survived, though badly wounded. Two of my team were wounded by shrapnel and were replaced. A reserve team was quickly deployed to take over but the event was unnerving. We had cleared about twenty-five metres when the same thing happened in the same lane. This time all five men were killed. Our own team stayed intact until an anti-personnel mine which had escaped clearance, detonated behind us. I was leading with the mine detector. Both men at the rear of the group survived but suffered severe lower body injuries. They were replaced from company reserves and we carried on. We had been working for about two hours, at which point we could have expected to be replaced by a fresh team but the plan was interrupted when we were suddenly subjected to incoming artillery fire. Two shells detonated mines in the ground ahead of us which added to the confusion. My confusion was stilled by sudden pain and the realisation that a fragment of shrapnel had cleanly removed my lower leg. My near team mate took a morphine syringe from his medical pack, plunged it into my thigh and I went to sleep. I woke up in a hospital bed a day later. My war was finished. I was told that my company had cleared the road after about eight hours work and that the tank attack was able to continue. I was also told that my company had lost another thirty-five men, killed or wounded during the night. My company had ceased to be a viable unit but we had done our duty. I understand that many members of my company are to receive bravery awards, including the dead. I have lost a leg but a bravery medal would be nice!

The story of a river crossing

Told to our Defence Correspondent at the Military Headquarters in Mogocha by Lieutenant Alexsandr Zhukov of 10th Engineer Pontoon Bridge Regiment, Arkhala, Amur Oblast. Part of 270th Demidov-Polotsk Motor Rifle Division (Khabarovsk).

A comment on this story – told by Alexsandr Zhukov

I have included this story, which is of a non-combat activity to highlight one of many essential activities that go on behind the front line. It is rather long but is a good example of the unsung support given to forward units.

My unit is equipped with the PMP: Pontoon Bridge Pack System. Our unit, of 350 men, deploys 80 plus logistic vehicles, which include 32 pontoon units, 12 tugboats and other pieces of equipment which can be assembled into a floating bridge of up to 382 metres long or 8 independent ferries. The bridge will then take weights of up to 50 tons, including all tanks in service spread at 30 metres apart when crossing. All our vehicles were standard wheeled logistic vehicles. The main element of our floating bridge, the pontoons, are lorry mounted. Each lorry carries a 10-metre long section of pontoon. Each pontoon lorry reverses down to the water's edge and launches its pontoon into the water. The pontoon automatically unfolds sideways into four linked sections which lock together. Each section forms a 10-metre length which can be joined to other sections to form a continuous bridge, or assembled in units of four pontoons to form a ferry.

After the Chinese invaded, we left our barracks and moved to an assembly area to the east of Khabarovsk to await further orders. We remained in our barracks and were very aware that our forces were in combat with the Chinese invaders to our east. About a week after the start of the war, our regiment was given the task of bridging the River Amur, placing our pontoon bridge close to the M60 road bridge and railway bridge. The aim was to provide additional road space to allow our retreating units to move to the west. The road system around Khabarovsk was already congested, and our first problem was moving our eighty or so vehicles out of our barracks and headed for our bridging site. It was important to ensure that the vehicles travelled in a planned sequence so that each unit arrived at the bridge site in a logical order to allow incremented construction. All vehicles were arranged in the correct sequence but, in the melee of traffic, the sequence was soon interrupted by other units' vehicles forcing their way into our column. We were able to identify and recover most of our vehicles at the point of access to our bridging site but, for some reason, we lost a few whose importance and loss was to be realised later.

It was very dark and raining heavily, and the launch site chosen by our reconnaissance party was already awash and very muddy. We managed to assemble our vehicles into some sort of order and began bridging operations. We had managed to persuade our sister engineer regiment to lend us two flexible roadway laying vehicles, which at least allowed reasonable access from our vehicle park to the pontoon launcher point and the first vehicle backed down to the river's edge. The bank was steep but we were able to launch our first load: a tugboat. These boats were used to tow pontoon sections to the crossing site and place upriver anchors. A secondary tugboat task was to hold station downriver to fish out any soldiers falling into the river. On the first launch came our first problem, which was the absence of anchors and cables which should have been in each pontoon section. The first pontoon had none; a checking fault which should have been picked up in barracks. Fortunately, following pontoons were properly equipped. We ended up with three safety tugs and six to perform towing and anchoring tasks.

Our next problem arose when we tried to drive the first launch vehicle away from the riverbank. The bank was far too steep. The vehicle ended up marooned in mud up to its chassis and had to be abandoned. This process was encountered many times. At the end of the launch phase, we had twenty vehicles buried in the riverbank. We rescued the remainder with much physical effort by soldiers who became very wet, mud covered and fed up.

About two months before the war, we had staged a demonstration of our bridging capability to a VIP audience at a pre-prepared site. They were very impressed by the completion of a 350-metre long bridge in 2½ hours, in daylight! In the end, the completion of our current task took 8 hours. Two major problems occurred during the build. The gods were not with us that night, and four complete pontoon sections had to be abandoned because, for some reason, the locking pins, which lock pontoon sections onto previously launched sections, refused to lock. After much effort and bad language, the complete sections had to be abandoned and allowed to escape downriver. As an example of bad practice, my commander found me trying to drive in a recalcitrant pin whilst my men stood around me. I was told off for not doing my proper job, overseeing the whole site, and told to leave it to my men. He was quite right.

The next problem arose when we came across a sandbank which did not leave enough water to allow pontoons to float. We had men in the water shovelling out silt into our tugboats to gain freeboard. That incident delayed progress by at least an hour and created another bunch of very wet, muddy and, by now, hungry soldiers. Two lucky soldiers, who fell off the bridge, were rescued by our safety boats.

The last construction problem was caused as a consequence of having lost, in the shambles of traffic chaos on the roads leading to the site, both entrance and exit ramps to the completed pontoon bridge. Our solution to that problem was to misuse two AVLBs: Armoured Vehicle Launched Bridges. These are of aluminium with a fixed span, in this case 30 metres, Type MTU-72, mounted on top of a T72 tank, which launch the bridge in one piece across any gap. The bridge had easy access ramps which could be used by wheeled and tracked vehicles, in the latter case weighing up to 50 tons. They were much longer than we needed but provided ramp access to and from the banks to allow vehicles to ride up onto the main bridge. Our bridge was intended to improve the rate of traffic flow heading west and we achieved this. Intended primarily for tracked vehicles, it was also occasionally used by wheeled vehicles, which in two or three cases misjudged the rather narrow ramps and flipped sideways off the bridge. Hold-ups were minimised by pushing the vehicles off the bridge into the water. Needs must.

Dragging anchors were a constant problem and we had to stay on site to correct these and any other problems which arose. We were therefore on site when the order came to either recover the bridge units or destroy them. This order was a consequence of the close approach of Chinese units and the requirement to remove our bridge and create gaps in the nearby road and railway bridges to slow the Chinese advance. We had insufficient time to recover our pontoon bridge, and the decision was made to destroy it. This involved placing explosive charges on the pin joints between selected sections, cutting the anchor cables, setting off the charges and letting the pontoon sections float away. Each pontoon was foam filled, so they just floated off downstream. The T72 bridge-laying tanks had departed, so their bridges went off with the pontoons. We sank the tugs.

My unit had carried out its allotted task and was left with no equipment with which to repeat the exercise. We loaded up our personal equipment and joined the remains of the 3rd Combined Combat Army retreating to the west.

Having left the bridging site, I reflected on the fact that we had suffered no casualties, although we had lost all our equipment. I suspect that the Chinese were aware of our activities but were assured of ultimate victory and were content to allow surviving Russian units to escape to the west and save themselves the trouble of containing them. We fared far better than our sister units in the Donbas and at Kherson, who suffered very high casualty rates and much loss of equipment when they carried out their river-crossing tasks.

Tanks used as artillery

A Day in the Life of Artemus Smirnov

I have been trained as a tank commander. Over half of my unit has been sent to fight in Ukraine as infantry soldiers, as there are not enough tanks remaining for them to use. Those of us remaining in Khabarovsk have the task of withdrawing from store all that remains of our tank reserves. All the T90s, 72s and 64s have been sent to Ukraine. All we have left in our store sheds are the rusting hulks of T62s built sixty years ago and finally withdrawn from service as they became a poor match for the British Chieftains, German Leopards and American M60 Pattons, which had powerful guns, thicker armour and superior mobility. Our stockpile of T62s have remained static for fifty years, although at least most had been motored a few hundred metres to check functionality.

So my unit withdrew twenty of what seemed to be the best of a very poor sample and prepared them for action. All were mobile, with turrets which moved through 360 degrees and 115mm guns which elevated up to 15 degrees. None of them had a coaxial machine gun in the turret or the 12.7mm gun normally mounted on the turret top. The worst aspect of their condition was that none had gun-aiming sights: telescopes and calibrators had been cannibalised for use on other tanks. The greatest shock to my unit was that we were not apparently expected to go into action as tanks but were to be used instead as artillery. A stockpile of high explosive rounds was available. These rounds did not have a large high explosive punch and would normally have been used against soft targets such as logistic vehicles and infantry defensive positions. Their effect on impact was far less than that achieved by 155mm artillery rounds, but they were useful against their expected target spectrum. The main problem with our tanks guns was how to use them in the absence of gun sights. A normal artillery gun would traverse and elevate to specific sight settings calculated to hit the target. Without sights, our ability was set initially by guesswork adjusted by observation of the achieved strike, by eyesight or from the air if, for instance, drones were available.

My unit was assigned to a combat group resisting the Chinese advance by deploying on the north bank of the River Amur. Map interpretation allowed us to identify a number of areas of woodland or urban development which might be useful for the enemy to use as harbour areas or areas of concentration prior to an attack. We spent a considerable amount of time and many rounds of ammunition to arrive at gun settings which allowed us to fire at these targets if required. We had to jury rig sights which allowed us to replicate firing settings if needed. We also had to be prepared to adjust these settings should we have to move our vehicles: quite possible given the amount of enemy air and drone activity observed. By keeping range settings reasonably constant, we could adjust traverse settings as required. We did as professional a job as was possible given the ridiculous task we were set, and were given firing orders to test our preparations.

Quite soon, we were involved in providing a heavy bombardment of an area of woodland where significant enemy activity was noticed. We soon experienced a major problem: the gun barrels on our tanks were already quite badly worn. The first tank to suffer had fired only about fifty rounds when a blowback occurred. In sequence, the projectile in the barrel no longer travelled smoothly up the worn bore. Projectiles began to vibrate as they were forced along the barrel by the propelling charge. If this vibration became too bad then a shell exploded within the barrel.

The visual effects were that the barrel disintegrated, with the front portion landing fifty metres in front of the tank. The gun breach mechanism was blown backwards into the turret. The combination of explosions of propelling charge and explosive round immediately ignited the rounds stored in the turret, leading to a massive explosion. The turret disintegrated and sprayed upwards and sideways around the tank. The hull centre also broke into fragments, together with the track and idling wheels. The tank was completely destroyed. If anyone had cared to look, they would have found only charred remains of the crew.

This massive explosive event was seen by other tank crews who recognised a failure caused by extreme overuse of a gun in a way which was never intended. Remaining tanks within the unit ceased firing immediately. The tanks had become unusable hulks, abandoned by the crews. The unit had ceased to exist.

The Chinese Army sits across the River Amur replete with modern equipment. We cannot defend ourselves with the dross of an army of the past. We will not prevail.

CHAPTER TWENTY

The EU Commission discusses with China the outcome of the War in Siberia

And asks for its cooperation in facilitating the arrangements proposed to end the conflict. China insists on the neutrality of Sibir

| *Exchanges between the EU Commissioner for Foreign Affairs and the Chinese Foreign Minister*

Exchanges between The EU Commissioner for Foreign Affairs and The Chinese Foreign Minister

Statement from the EU Commissioner

From our Defence Correspondent

1. The EU supported China's desire and intention to reverse the unfair Treaty of Aigun. This support did not apply to China's military aggressive method of achieving that goal. We had wished that negotiations between Russia and China would have led to a satisfactory outcome. Russia is a European country and we support its resistance to any attempt by China to recover more territory than was lost as a consequence of Aigun. There is uncertainty in establishing the boundaries in Siberia of the Chinese state prior to Aigun. The EU accepts that the Russian Empire was at its most predatory in the mid 19th century and we therefore believe that significant territory had been lost by China prior to the Treaty of Aigun. Our cartographers and historians believe that Lake Baikal would have been a natural boundary for Chinese people moving west, in the same way as the lake would have been a natural boundary for Russians

moving east. I therefore suggest to you that Lake Baikal becomes the new international boundary between China and Russia, stretching to the River Lena, one hundred kilometres south of Yakutsk, then east to the Okhotsk Sea.

2. The EU has always been concerned about the rights of ethnic peoples who are frequently ignored by more powerful countries, especially those seeking territory by expansion. It is especially true when considering the ethnic groups who populated Siberia before China and Russia expanded into their space. These groups could not defend their rights given the overwhelming power of China and Russia. The majority of members of the UN, who will at some stage be asked to recognise your presence in East Siberia, will therefore look favourably on the proposal, which the EU will put forward, that these numerous but related groups are encouraged to form a Federation of Nations in mid-Siberia. This land would lie to the west, between Lake Baikal and the proposed new Russian border to the east of the Ural Mountains, bordered in the east by your now reclaimed territory and in the north by the Arctic Sea. These groups must name their own country, but for the time being I suggest that we call it Sibir. This has historic significance, stretching between the Mongolia border in the south and the Arctic in the north. Sibir was the name given to the land east of the Urals, stretching into mid-Siberia by the Khanates, who were the descendants of the Mongols, who captured the territory in the 13th/14th centuries.

3. NATO forces are now occupying land between Mongolia and Lake Baikal. I believe that the land to the east of Baikal and to its north represents all you would have wished to occupy to correct Aigun. I trust that the proposal I have outlined and shown on the maps I present to you will meet your strategic aims and that a conflict with NATO forces would not be contemplated by China.

4. In the context of territorial claims, the EU also wishes to raise with China territorial issues with countries that supported China in the UN General Assembly vote on Aigun but with which China is in dispute.

The EU is conscious of:

a. Your dispute with India over areas of Ladakh and also of Uttar Pradesh. The EU is concerned that conflicts in these areas could affect neighbouring countries and therefore world peace adversely. The EU very much hopes that you will be able to solve these disputes amicably and quickly.

b. The EU is also very concerned about your militarisation of large areas of the South China Sea. A number of countries on the periphery of the sea have claims against you upheld in international law concerning areas affecting their immediate sea environment. There is particular concern over the extent to which you are claiming jurisdiction of international waters which carry a very large proportion of international trade. The EU cannot accept this acquisition of authority where none previously existed. The EU requests the demilitarisation of the South China Sea and the restoration of regard for international law over the entire area.

I would like to point out that recognition of your new international boundaries in eastern Siberia will require the consent of a majority of UN members, and this might not be forthcoming if China is seen to be ignoring international law with which they are all expected to comply. The EU will continue to support the justifiable reversion of the unfair terms of the Treaty of Aigun in the manner described above, so long as China is seen to abide by the principles of international law on which that claim rests. Otherwise, the EU will not recognise or assist you in reaching agreement on your new Siberian boundaries. We are prepared to go further and say that we would, in consultation with and agreement of those countries concerned, place impediments in your way should you disregard their wishes.

From The Chinese Foreign Minister

Thank you for your communication. First, let me say that China has a major objection to the EU deciding where China's borders lie. I note that, in mitigation, the EU did support at the UN China's claim and reasonable action to be taken to restore China's integrity. China has no wish to take military action beyond what is necessary to correct Aigun. You have raised specific issues which we will address. Meanwhile, China has no interest in confronting NATO forces. You can be assured that China's forces deployed in Siberia will remain in their present positions whilst the issues concerned are discussed. China wishes to live in peace with the EU and contemplates an amicable resolution of the current problems. We are also anxious to live in peace with our neighbours in the South China Sea, and we will discuss with them the problems that you raise. There are, however, certain assurances which we seek which China requires to be fulfilled before we indicate broad agreement to your proposals. These assurances are required to protect China from any possibility that a hostile power will in any way threaten China from the West through Sibir.

1. The state of Sibir must not conclude any treaties with other states which are of a military nature.
2. No NATO, Russian or any other nation's military units will be garrisoned in Sibir after the expiration of a maximum of five years after the conclusion and ratification of the agreement by all interested parties.
3. Sibir will not be permitted to create air or naval forces. Forces required to maintain law and order and to protect its borders will be of a size agreed by parties to this agreement and will be armed with small arms and matching lightly armoured vehicles only.
4. China and NATO will maintain monitoring organisations of agreed size with responsibility to liaise with the Sibir Government and brief nations party to this agreement of any deviation from the terms of this agreement.
5. China will wish to work with the EU in carrying out the terms of the agreement to assist in the establishment of this new state. The mandate given to the EU should not run for more than five years.

China wishes to see a stable nation on its border and will work with the EU to create this circumstance.

Further comment by The EU Foreign Affairs Commissioner

Thank you for your comments, which I am sure will be the cause of considerable discussion between China, the EU and all other interested parties, including the USA. For the moment, the EU wishes to pause discussions and actions, but it does wish to reinforce a view, supported by the USA, that the issues which we have highlighted in relation to China's foreign policy must be settled by international agreement before either the

EU or the USA or, I believe, the UN would be able to support China's acquisition of new territory in Siberia and that the imposition of sanctions would follow should agreement not be reached.

Comment by our Defence Editor
The diplomatic exchanges between the EU and Chinese representatives indicate a meeting of minds in relation to the ongoing war. The exchanges need to be translated into inter-government agreements. There is every reason to expect agreement to be reached.

IN THIS CASE, THE WAR IS OVER
THE USA AND CHINA MUST NOW TALK

SIBERIA NATIONAL BOUNDARIES ON THE CONCLUSION OF THE RUSSIA / CHINA WAR

World Peace – A reinvigorated United Nations

A joint paper by China Forward and New Europe

The terms of the unfair treaties imposed on China in 1858/60 have now been reversed. China has gained a large area of East Siberia, which gives it geostrategic security. Russia has abandoned its imperial ambitions and also the large sweep of Siberian territory which it had found impossible to control. Russia has retired to within borders linked to its historic past. It has surrendered territory previously part of east European countries which it had acquired by political/military pressure. Russia is now geographically, culturally and economically part of Europe.

We believe that these actions have created an opportunity for a re-ordering of world politics, with the hope that a world at peace can be achieved. We make a plea to the four main centres of power in the world to work to resolve their differences within the framework of the United Nations. We are addressing: China, the United States of America, the European Union and India.

The UN Security Council has very seldom been able to perform the function for which it was formed: the creation of stability amongst nations by force of argument, economic pressure and, if necessary, military might. Too many of the permanent members of the Security Council were themselves seen to have irreconcilable ambitions and positions which prevented agreement on many issues. Russia has now left the Council. We propose:

1. That the permanent members of the Security Council are reduced to five – China, USA, India, the EU and Japan.
2. That the veto powers of the five permanent members are removed.
3. That six additional Council members will be chosen on a rotational basis, for instance, by one member being changed every six months. These rotational members would be chosen by international agreement of members of four regional groupings:
   a. Pacific
   b. Atlantic

      c. South East Asia

      d. Africa: plus:

      e. Two non-aligned, chosen by the General Assembly

4. That the Security Council should be chaired by the Secretary General of the UN. Motions put to it will be decided by a majority vote to include agreement by at least two of the permanent members.

5. The Secretary General of the UN should also chair a permanent working party with members chosen from the same groupings as above. This working party will act as a filter, proposing problems to the Security Council as they arise.

We ask that the five permanent members recognise that a unique opportunity has arisen to establish and maintain world peace and to shed the nationalistic hubris which has caused so much damage in the past. The President of Russia's personal hubris and nationalistic fervour led to Russia's unforgivable actions in Crimea and Ukraine. Such situations should not be permitted to reoccur.

Please do not waste this opportunity.

Narrative Ends: Actions Now Required

The narrative suggests the principal arrangements for the reordering of Siberia but leaves many issues to be decided and agreed at the highest level. The principal issues concerned are listed below, culminating in decisions to be taken within the United Nations:

International Borders

Russia cedes:

- Aigun-based territory to China
- North East Siberia to USA
- Central Siberia to Sibir

Russia relinquishes control over:

- Kaliningrad
- Transnistria
- Annexed Ukraine land, including Crimea
- Abkhazia and South Ossetia in Georgia
- Eastern Moldova
- Sakhalin and Kurils

Russia concedes independence to:

- Ingushetia
- Dagestan
- Chechnya
- Other minor Caucasian republics
- and will support the renewed independence of Belarus.

Population Movements

- Sibir Federal State absorbs Siberiaks and original ethnic groups.
- East Siberian Siberiaks are integrated into new Chinese territory, or move by choice.
- Territory annexed by Russia post 1945 should revert to parent nations. Population movements may be necessary.

Democratisation of Russia

- The President of Russia now gone.
- Interim government, leading to new elections.
- Major reductions of military establishment and nuclear arsenal.
- Initiation of process to allow Russia to join the EU and NATO.
- Russia is to agree to arrangements for payment of repartitions to Ukraine.

Maintenance of Stability in New Siberia

The EU Commission will seek from the United Nations a mandate with which it will associate China's involvement, to provide governance and security to Sibir to enable the formation of state institutions including finance and law and order, and will seek approval to maintain NATO forces within Sibir to facilitate the mandate for an agreed limited period. The overall aim will be to allow complete independence as soon as possible.

Actions Required by China

China is aware that acceptance of the existence of their new territory is subject to the approval of the United Nations. China has been encouraged to accept that this agreement will only be approved subsequent to China working with relevant nations to agree and settle geopolitical issues concerning India and the South China Sea. In particular, it is anticipated that the threatened invasion of Taiwan will have, at least, been postponed and hopefully abandoned.

Agreement of The United Nations

The considerable turmoil occasioned by Russia's adventure in Ukraine and China's incursion into East Siberia raises many issues, summarised above, which should be agreed by a vote in the General Assembly of the United Nations. It is anticipated that the Security Council, with an enhanced staff, will assume responsibility for the coordination of the issues raised and their eventual successful conclusion.

What Happens Next?

The story told in this book involves four political entities: the Russian Federation, the European Union including NATO, the People's Republic of China, the United States of America and India, collectively representing sixty-six percent of the world land area and fourty-five percent of its population. The book's premise is based on the realities of the Treaties of Aigun and Peking and the invasion of Ukraine by Russia. The book projects these realities into a fictional account of the conflict which these realities inspire.

Russia loses its empire and most of its Siberian hinterland and returns to its historic entity as a European country with ambitions to join the EU and NATO.

China recovers its lost lands and more in eastern Siberia but is enjoined to restrain its imperialist and expansionist policies including the potential invasion of Taiwan, to obtain international acceptance of its new territories.

Sibir The new, very large Republic of Sibir has to create its own internal institutions to gain international recognition and integrate its wide range of ethnic populations. The UN authorises a mandate to the EU Commission to provide initial governance and security to facilitate independence. The EU has to recognise China's interests in the functions of the mandate and accommodate them as far as practicable.

The United States of America has to absorb its new territory and assimilate and protect the ethnic groups within it.

The Security Council, led by the Secretary General of the United Nations, has to act as the coordinator of United Nations activities to gain acceptance of the new geopolitical circumstances in which Siberia now finds itself, to ensure that this vast area is allowed to settle into its new situation. It must also facilitate talks to be held between the People's Republic of China and the United States of America.

Epilogue: A Review of The Strategic Implications of The Russian/Chinese War

A Paper by New Europe

The Russian President's invasion of Ukraine had long been forecast by the President himself but regarded by the West as bluff. Its realisation was very unwelcome. It is to the credit of EU/NATO that its response was rapid: on moral grounds and to uphold international standards of law and order given Europe's recent history of turmoil. The invasion was accompanied by expressions of immediate concern from the Baltic states and Poland. The President was openly stating that the restoration of the defunct Soviet Empire was a geopolitical aim and that countries on its borders, previously part of the USSR, would be targeted. These concerns were recognised within EU/NATO and reinforced the growing determination to resist Russian aggression.

These realities morphed into a longer-term strategic plan reinforced by the demonstrated inability of the Russian Army to prevail against Ukraine. NATO planners now saw the possibility of Ukraine not just holding the Russian invaders but of defeating the Russians in combat and reducing what had been thought of as a superpower to one incapable of carrying out the President's long-term plans. Such a defeat would also raise questions within China on the capabilities of its alleged strategic partner. The downgrading of Russia's perceived capability could have a significant impact on China's ambitions. China would not have wanted Russia to be defeated in this way. EU/NATO had to persuade China to desist from providing military support to Russia, principally by threat of economic, financial and trade penalties if it did. This pressure worked. Russia had to retire into its homeland: imperial expansion become impossible, relying on an army shown to be no match for western technology, efficiently used.

Russia's economy was being seriously damaged by huge expenditure on its war, a lack of sophisticated technology and by trade and financial sanctions. Its people were being damaged by economic hardship, increasing levels of oppression and gloom following an obvious national humiliation. Russia would not now be regarded as a threat to western Europe, at least in the short term. However, in time, given continued internal social oppression and massive diversion of national wealth to rearmament, resurrection of imperial ambition could not be discounted. Some protection against this eventuality was provided by NATO's continued provision of protection to Ukraine against missile or projectile attack, including the destruction of initiating weapons. It was also necessary to provide formal cover against renewed aggression by hastening Ukraine's journey to becoming a full member of NATO. As a consequence, Russia's entire western border would be controlled by NATO, even, eventually, including Belarus. Thus, the position in eastern Europe stabilised: Ukraine was protected against further material damage and from further invasion by membership of NATO. Poland and the Baltic states remained protected. Russia reverted to its original heartlands and could in time revert to democracy.

This stability was again thrown into instability by China's invasion of East Siberia. China now regarded Russia as a very poor protector of its far western border. Russia had shown itself to be a nation with less economic and military capability than it had claimed. China required long-term stability on its western border and sought it through invasion. It already had a motive based on its desire to reclaim the lands lost by the Treaty of Aigun. The recovery of that land had increasingly become a subject of debate within China. Its vocal protagonists now had a further reason to press their views. These views were noted in Europe, but action to activate them had not been expected. China's invasion into East Siberia came as a surprise. Given Russia's battered condition, immediate concern was expressed as to Russia's ability to withstand China's aggression. The prospect of China on its eastern flank gave western Europe its own potential problem. This view was reinforced by the extraordinary plea for help from Russia, seeking support to resist the intruder. This position was a complete reversal of the Ukraine situation but was immediately recognised as one which had to be addressed, and support provided as requested. EU/NATO saw this as an opportunity to encourage the impending movement of Russia into its European continental heartland and was therefore to be welcomed.

The involvement of EU/NATO in this way reinforced the evident benefits to Europe which had emerged from its consistent support provided to Ukraine. It could finally be claimed that the whole of Europe, including Russia, had achieved a level of internal national coexistence which had never been previously achieved. China benefitted from land acquisition but, more importantly, achieved a restabilised western border with a new state: SIBIR. This very large and passive nation provided a cushion of protection which, nevertheless, required China to divert significant military resources to secure its new border. A negative aspect of China's acquisition was that the USA now had a new land border in Siberia, separated by only a few hundred kilometres from China's north-eastern border. In any confrontation with the USA in the Indo-Pacific, China now had to consider the potential of military activity on two fronts. This possibility would inevitably lower the probability of Chinese aggression.

The EU/NATO support given to Ukraine was based on a strategic plan which achieved more success than could initially have been imagined: Ukraine, heading for membership of NATO and the EU, was spared any further assault from Russia; Poland and the Baltic states continued to enjoy security within NATO. China had regained its lost territory and a stabilised western border, and the USA had gained territory in north-eastern Siberia.

Russia had lost a large part of its Siberian empire and could finally settle down as a natural part of the European continent, with a reasonable prospect of becoming increasingly democratic and economically stable. For Russia, imperial ambitions no longer held any attraction. China had stabilised its northern borders but at the cost of reducing its own imperial ambitions in the Indo-Pacific region. There was at least a chance that all the powers involved in Ukraine and its aftermath conflict in Siberia could now be content with their new circumstances and re-establish peaceful coexistence.

The Story of New Siberia has Just Started

DAVID W. WILLIAMS, O.B.E., BSc (Econ) and
Chartered Engineer
Colonel (Retired)

David Williams was born in 1935 – old enough
in February 1941 to watch the Luftwaffe engage
with the RAF in dog fights over his home town:
Swansea. He has memories of walking over
firehose pipes playing on burning buildings in
the devastated city centre. He went on to attend
Gowerton Grammar School from where, to the surprise of his peers and
headmaster, he was accepted into The Royal Military Academy, Sandhurst
as an officer cadet. He was commissioned as a subaltern into the Royal
Engineers on 4th February 1955.

In his early commissioned years he commanded units which built roads
and bridges in Malaysia, a Wilderness park in Canada and a Sports Stadium
in Gibraltar. He also served tours in the 12 Infantry Brigade as part of the
British Army of the Rhine confronting the Warsaw Pact armies headed by
the Soviet Union.

As a Major, he attended Technical and General Staff Colleges and was
also nominated to attend the National Defence College. This process was
interrupted by the advent of miliary tuberculosis and leukemia, leading to a
break of two years from active service.

As a Lieutenant Colonel and Colonel he lectured on the strategy and
tactics of nuclear warfare and served in General Staff appointments
concerned with a weapon design and procurement. Ill health returned in
the form of pneumonia and meningitis and he was discharged prematurely
from service in 1988.

For the next 25 years he started and ran a furniture manufacturing
Company from which he retired in 2015. Along the way he suffered colon
cancer and a stroke. He is now a partner in a family-owned vineyard. His
wife died of very late diagnosed cancer in 2021. He remains healthy and
retains an interest in international economic and military matters

He was a contributing author to *The Third World War: A Future History* by
General Sir John Hackett published in 1979.

Milton Keynes UK
Ingram Content Group UK Ltd.
UKHW020218160324
439478UK00002B/2